PIPPA'S
iSLAND

BOOKS BY BELINDA MURRELL

Pippa's Island
Book 1: The Beach Shack Cafe
Book 2: Cub Reporters

The Locket of Dreams
The Ruby Talisman
The Ivory Rose
The Forgotten Pearl
The River Charm
The Sequin Star
The Lost Sapphire

The Sun Sword Trilogy
Book 1: The Quest for the Sun Gem
Book 2: The Voyage of the Owl
Book 3: The Snowy Tower

Lulu Bell
Lulu Bell and the Birthday Unicorn
Lulu Bell and the Fairy Penguin
Lulu Bell and the Cubby Fort
Lulu Bell and the Moon Dragon
Lulu Bell and the Circus Pup
Lulu Bell and the Sea Turtle
Lulu Bell and the Tiger Cub
Lulu Bell and the Pyjama Party
Lulu Bell and the Christmas Elf
Lulu Bell and the Koala Joey
Lulu Bell and the Arabian Nights
Lulu Bell and the Magical Garden
Lulu Bell and the Pirate Fun

BOOK 1

PIPPA'S ISLAND

THE BEACH SHACK CAFE

BELINDA MURRELL

RANDOM HOUSE AUSTRALIA

A Random House book
Published by Penguin Random House Australia Pty Ltd
Level 3, 100 Pacific Highway, North Sydney NSW 2060
www.penguin.com.au

 Penguin
Random House
Australia

First published by Random House Australia in 2017

Addresses for the Penguin Random House group of companies can be found at
global.penguinrandomhouse.com/offices.

National Library of Australia
Cataloguing-in-Publication entry

Creator: Murrell, Belinda, author
Title: The beach shack cafe / Belinda Murrell
ISBN: 978 0 14378 367 1 (pbk)
Series: Murrell, Belinda. Pippa's Island; 1
Target audience: For primary school age
Subjects: New schools – Juvenile fiction
           Coffee shops – Juvenile fiction
           Island life – Juvenile fiction

Cover and internal design by Christabella Designs
Cover and internal images: beautiful white beach Charcompix/Shutterstock;
lemon cupcakes Marharyta Kovalenko/Shutterstock; portrait of a young girl
Andrey Arkusha/Shutterstock; a spotted dolphin family Paulphin Photography/
Shutterstock; young woman kayaking Beth Swanson/Shutterstock; summer
cards Ksenia Lokko/Shutterstock; hand-drawn summer creative alphabet
Ksenia Lokko/Shutterstock
Typeset by Midland Typesetters, Australia
Printed in Australia by Griffin Press, an accredited ISO AS/NZS 14001:2004
Environmental Management System printer

Penguin Random House Australia uses papers that are natural, renewable
and recyclable products and made from wood grown in sustainable forests.
The logging and manufacturing processes are expected to conform to the
environmental regulations of the country of origin.

For Pippa Masson and Zoe Walton for
all your wisdom, encouragement and
bookish genius. Thank you. I'd never have
written this series without you!
And for Pepper Abercrombie — may all
your dreams bring you joy.

Have you ever heard of Kira Island? I didn't think so. Not many people have. If you look at the postcards it looks like a tropical paradise. White sandy beaches, coral-fringed reefs, frangipanis and palm trees, sparkling turquoise water and dolphins splashing in the waves. I know, it sounds like heaven.

But that's definitely not what I thought when Mum announced we were moving there. I loved my life in London. Our big old terrace house. My gang of gorgeous friends. My school. Horseriding lessons in Hyde Park. Playing hockey on Saturdays and shopping trips to Oxford Street. So of course I didn't want to leave.

Which brings me to Mum's crazy idea. One day, she decided to pack up everything, pull the three of us out of school and move to the other side of the world, to a tiny tropical island called Kira Island. My grandparents live there and it's where Mum grew up.

Not only that, but Mum decided to spend every penny we had on a tumbledown, derelict boatshed. Her grand dream was to renovate it and turn it into an arty bookshop cafe. The place was so bad that the first time we went there, I put my foot right through the floor. It was awful!

To save money, we've been living in an old caravan in the back garden of my grandparents' cottage. Me, Mum, my brother Harry and my little sister Bella have all been jammed into a space smaller than my old bedroom back home.

You can probably see why I wasn't super-happy about the move. In fact, Mum later said I had been particularly **recalcitrant**, which apparently means difficult or stubborn.

So on my first day at my brand-new school, when I met the girls, I was certain I was living through the second-worst day of my life. I didn't know **anyone**.

Back then, I had no idea how much fun I was going to have. Or how these three girls were going to become my best friends.

So this is the story of a gang of girls. Charlie Harper, Meg O'Loughlin, Cici Lin and, of course, me, Philippa Elizabeth Hamilton. Otherwise known as

Pippa

CHAPTER 1

FIRST DAY

Kira Cove Primary School. It seemed a world away from the friends and school I left behind just a few weeks ago. My uniform smelled new and starchy. When I walked through the school gate, I felt a teensy bit scared. Actually, extremely scared! No one likes starting at a new school, do they? I wondered if the kids would be nice. Would I make friends? Would my teacher like me?

A lady from the office took me into the classroom, introduced me to the teacher, Mrs Marshall, and left me there.

The kids all took advantage of the interruption to chat and laugh. Mrs Marshall shushed them with just a glance. She seemed stern and I hoped she wasn't going to be too mean.

I stood in front of a sea of strange faces, all of them staring at me. The faces blurred into one another. Boys and girls, wearing the same blue-and-white uniforms. To say I was feeling nervous was an understatement. I had butterflies doing somersaults in my tummy.

'Class 5M, I'd like to introduce Philippa Hamilton, who has recently arrived from London,' she said. 'This is her first day at Kira Cove School so I hope you will welcome her warmly.'

A girl at the back of the classroom whispered something to the girls she was sitting with. They all giggled. I felt myself blushing. I glared down at my squeaky, shiny black school shoes. It was horrible having everyone stare at me.

'Please say good morning, class,' said Mrs Marshall.

'Good morning, Phil-lip-pa,' chanted the whole class.

'Good morning, 5M,' I mumbled. Did my voice give a tell-tale wobble? 'I'm Philippa but everyone calls me Pippa.'

'Olivia, could you please sit up the back next to Connor?' asked Mrs Marshall. 'And Philippa – I mean Pippa – you can take a seat there next to Meg.'

A girl stood up and packed away her books. She didn't look very happy about changing seats. I slid into her empty chair and looked around. On my left was a girl with blue eyes and bobbed, honey-brown hair. On my right was a girl with long, blonde, wavy hair, green eyes and a sprinkle of freckles on her nose. Honey-girl smiled at me, in a shy kind of way.

'Hi, Pippa,' she whispered. 'I'm Meg O'Loughlin.'

The other girl leant over with a dazzling smile. 'And I'm Charlie.'

'Hi,' I replied quietly, glancing down at my lap.

'If you're quite finished, girls, we'll continue with our maths,' said Mrs Marshall. She sounded gruff but I noticed her eyes looked kind.

The morning fell into a familiar pattern of maths, spelling and reading. I doodled pictures of flowers and dogs and love hearts in the margin of my exercise book while the others marked their homework.

When the recess bell rang, the whole class raced for the door. It was chaos in the corridor as everyone searched in their schoolbags for hats and snacks. I finally reached my bag, where

I'd left it hanging on a hook, and dug out my own hat and lunch box. I joined the stream of students pouring into the playground.

Outside, kids were running, shouting, playing and laughing. If I closed my eyes it sounded just like the playground of my old school back in London. But instead of cool and misty air, the sun shone down bright and hot. The air smelled different too. All sea-salty and spicy. And of course the biggest difference was that almost everyone was a stranger.

Back home, I'd been with the same group of kids since we started nursery school at the age of three. I'd known every student in the whole school. My best friends were Miranda, Ava and Lily, and I missed them terribly. My prep school, Bromley House, was in a beautiful old red-brick mansion, near the River Thames. There was a walled garden out the back where we would play. Lunch was always served in the dining hall, which had a high-pitched beamed

ceiling and oak panelling. We'd sit at our favourite table and chat as we ate a hot meal of pasta
or chicken with vegetables. It couldn't have
been more different.

Here, the school buildings were dazzling-
white with wide, shady verandas. Hot-pink
bougainvillea flowers twisted around the posts
and tumbled over the roof. And the playground
seemed huge.

I hesitated, not sure what to do. I didn't
know whether to sit with some kids from my
class, or go and find a hidden place to skulk
by myself. Or perhaps I should look for Harry
and Bella, and make sure they were all right.

A moment later, I saw my little sister's trade-
mark corkscrew curls. She ran past, surrounded
by a group of year one kids, and with a huge
smile on her face. Bella was obviously fine.

'Hi, Bella,' I called. 'Have you seen Harry?'

Bella didn't pause but just kept running.
'He's playing football,' she yelled. 'Over there.'

A big crowd of year four kids was kicking a ball around. My brother was a super-keen football player. I saw him racing around, chasing the ball and hooting with laughter. Clearly Harry was perfectly happy too.

It didn't seem to have taken either of them any time at all to make friends.

It was then that I saw Meg waiting for me. She waved me over timidly.

'I thought you might like to come and sit with us,' she said. 'Most of the year fives meet under that tree over there.'

At the far end of the playground was a huge old tree with spreading branches. A group of students was sitting in the shade.

'Thanks,' I said, with relief. 'That would be great.'

We started walking together side by side.

'Was that your little sister?' Meg asked quietly. She seemed shy but she was making an effort to be friendly. 'She looks like you.'

My grandmother Mimi says that Harry, Bella and I are like three peas in a pod, which apparently means we all look alike – wild, curly brown hair, chocolate-brown eyes and skin the colour of caramel.

I nodded. 'Bella's six. She likes to pretend she's a dinosaur, which usually involves a lot of roaring and stomping. And I have a brother, Harry, who's nine and the quietest one in the family.'

Meg laughed. 'I have a brother too, Jack, but he's older. He's in year six. When did you move here?'

I felt my tummy do the somersault thing again. 'A few weeks ago. We had a holiday while Mum organised everything. We're staying with my grandparents until our new place is ready.'

Meg looked at me with sympathy. 'Moving is tough, isn't it? My family moved to Kira Island a couple of years ago. It took a while to settle in, but it's great now.'

'Didn't you like it when you first moved here either?' I asked.

Meg grinned and shook her head. 'I hated it! Especially going to school, because I'd never been before. But I got used to it.'

'Really, you hadn't been to school?' Starting over at a different school was hard enough. I couldn't imagine what it would be like to face your first day ever somewhere new.

'My mum's a marine biologist so we travelled around a lot when we were younger and did home-schooling. She studies whales and dolphins in the wild. But then Mum decided we needed to go to a proper school, so she took a job here at Marine Animal Rescue Service. We live on a yacht in the harbour.'

'I've never met anyone who lives on a boat.' All my friends in London lived in big terrace houses just like ours. 'Isn't it squishy?'

'A bit,' agreed Meg cheerfully. 'But I'm used to it.'

'Wow. That's fantastic.' I realised that living on a boat couldn't be too different to living in a caravan, like my family was. I began to feel a lot better about moving and starting a new school. Maybe I could make new friends and do fun things too.

We reached the big tree. A group of nine girls was sitting cross-legged in a rough circle, nibbling happily at the food from their lunch boxes. Two of the girls wriggled over to make room for us.

Meg sat down between them. I sat next to her, feeling self-conscious all over again with everyone looking at us. I pulled my skirt down straight.

Meg waved towards the two girls who had made room for us. One was the blonde-haired girl who I'd been sitting next to. The other was the Chinese girl who'd sat on the other side of Meg. She was one of the prettiest girls I'd ever seen, with straight black hair, a thick fringe and brown eyes.

'You met Charlie already, and this is Cici,' said Meg.

We said hi, then I looked around at the other girls in the circle.

'That's Olivia,' said Meg, pointing to the girl who'd had to move seats for me. 'And Willow, Eve, Jemila, Ariana, Tash and Sienna.'

They all murmured hellos and looked at me curiously. How would I ever remember who was who? Willow had brown plaits, green eyes and a snub nose. Sienna looked very athletic, or was that Tash?

'Did you really come from London?' asked Olivia. Her long dark hair was swept up into a high ponytail. She smiled at me in a friendly way. 'It must be an amazing place to live.'

Memories of my old home crowded in. 'Yes, I loved it. We lived in Chelsea before we moved here.'

Olivia twirled her hair around her finger. 'My mum's a marketing manager and she visits

London every year for her work. I've been with her twice. It's one of my favourite cities in the world.'

I warmed to Olivia at once. Anyone who loved my old hometown must be my sort of girl.

We chatted for a couple of minutes about what she'd done on her trips – high tea at Harrods, visits to the theatre and shopping on Oxford Street.

'Oxford Street is the most amazing place to shop,' I said. 'You could spend all day there and still not see everything.'

'Mum bought me some really cool outfits there,' said Olivia.

'London has the most fantastic fashion,' said Cici enthusiastically. 'I'd love to go.'

'Cici's mum is a fashion designer,' explained Meg. 'She and Cici are mad about clothes.'

It felt comforting to be talking to these new girls about familiar things. Maybe I *could* make friends here.

When everyone had finished their snacks, the group split up. Some of the girls raced over to the handball courts, while others joined a soccer game. I drifted along to the grassy lawn, where Olivia, Tash, Sienna and Willow threw themselves into a series of spectacular cartwheels and handstands. Tash could do sixty-seven cartwheels in a row!

The bell rang for the end of recess, and we joined the others.

'Ugghh,' said Charlie, scrunching up her face. 'We have a maths quiz now.'

Olivia walked beside me. The other girls trailed along behind. 'Mrs Marshall loves giving us super-hard maths quizzes.'

'It's all right for you, Olivia,' said Cici. 'You top the class every time.'

'Not just in maths quizzes,' said Meg, turning to me. 'Olivia got the academic prize for our class last year.'

Olivia gave a little skip. 'Well, I like maths.'

'Me too,' I said. Olivia and I smiled at each other. It looked like we had a lot in common. She seemed exactly the sort of girl I'd like to be friends with.

CHAPTER 2

MATHS QUIZ

Olivia was right. The maths quiz was super-hard. But luckily, I'm pretty good at maths. I whizzed through the paper, chewing my pen while I thought about the hardest questions.

At the end of the quiz, we had to swap papers. Mrs Marshall read out the correct response and we had to mark each other's answers. I swapped with Charlie, while Meg swapped with Cici.

'Mine will be terrible,' Charlie complained. 'I'm just not good at maths.'

Charlie's paper was covered in scribbles and crossing out. She was definitely not good at maths, as I discovered. She barely passed.

'Told you,' whispered Charlie as I handed back her paper. 'But you did brilliantly.'

'Thanks,' I said, quickly checking the score.

I felt a rush of pride when I noticed that I'd only got one sum wrong.

Mrs Marshall gathered up the papers and shuffled through them to check the results.

'Well done, everyone,' said Mrs Marshall. 'And it looks like we have a new maths star in our class. Congratulations to Pippa for getting nearly full marks.'

Lots of the kids looked over at me. Charlie patted me on the back. But then I noticed that Olivia was glaring at me as if I was a nasty spider she had discovered in her bedroom. I looked away, feeling uncomfortable. What had I done?

After maths, Mrs Marshall split us up into groups of four to start work on a new science project. In my group was Meg, Charlie and Cici. Olivia was in a group with Willow, Tash and Sienna. Olivia looked over at our group as though she wished she was with us. I guess she would have been if Mrs Marshall hadn't moved her.

We had to design a game or toy made out of recycled materials. We started by sketching concepts in our science notebooks, brain-storming ideas and discussing names. It was fun.

Cici kept making the most ridiculous suggestions, just to make us giggle. 'I've got it! How about a game where each player has to set out on a world quest to find the perfect handbag?'

'We could call it Handbag Heaven!' I joked.

Cici flashed her fingernails, which were painted summery turquoise. 'Or the perfect nail colour?'

'Nail Nirvana!' said Charlie.

'Or how about Shoetopia?' suggested Cici.

'To see how many pairs of divine shoes you could collect along the way?'

The three of us laughed out loud. Mrs Marshall glanced at us. We quietened down immediately.

Meg huffed in disgust. 'You guys are not taking this seriously. How about a quest game where the players have to try to save endangered animals like African elephants, mountain gorillas or black rhinoceros?'

My ears pricked up. My parents had gone on safari in Tanzania for their honeymoon. I loved the stories Mum had told me and the beautiful photos she'd taken of elephants and other African animals in the wild. 'That sounds like a good plan.'

'Or why don't we just set up a racing track for toy cars to zip around?' suggested Charlie. 'That would be dead simple. I could recycle my brother's toys off the floor, so I don't have to step on them!'

At the end of the lesson, we'd made no progress at all. At this rate we'd never get our project done.

'Looks like we'll need to have a team meeting after school one afternoon,' said Charlie.

'I'll make the cupcakes,' said Cici. 'Lemon or strawberry-and-vanilla?'

'Lemon's my favourite,' said Meg.

'Are you in, Pippa?' asked Charlie.

I beamed at the girls. 'Definitely.' An after-school team meeting with lemon cupcakes and lots of laughs sounded absolutely perfect.

'We could meet at my house tomorrow after-noon?' suggested Charlie. 'But my house is the furthest from school, so maybe we'd be better to go to one of yours?'

'Mum works from home, and she has a big deadline this week so my place is out,' said Cici. 'Maybe we could meet at Pippa's? Where do you live?'

I thought of our tiny, crowded caravan in

the back garden of my grandparents' cottage. Then the messy, ruined boatshed. I didn't feel like having the girls over to either place.

I shook my head. 'We're staying with my grandparents at the moment so that probably won't work.'

'That's okay,' said Meg. 'You can come to our yacht.'

Mrs Marshall came over to check our progress. 'Are you settling in all right, Pippa?' she asked.

'Yes, Mrs Marshall,' I replied.

'And have you girls come up with a good plan for your project yet?' She looked right at me.

'Ah, yes.' I glanced around quickly at the other girls. They looked at me with panicked expressions. Clearly none of us wanted to tell Mrs Marshall about our frivolous ideas for a handbag quest! What could I say? I didn't want my new teacher to think we had wasted the whole lesson being silly. Then I remembered Meg's idea.

'We thought we'd design a quest game where the players have to cross an African plain,' I said. 'It would be a fun game, where players also learned how to save endangered animals . . . like elephants and rhinos.'

Mrs Marshall nodded. 'Sounds good – tell me more.'

My stressed brain started firing with ideas. 'The players would roll the dice and meet challenges like . . . like catching hunters or wildlife smugglers. They could pick up cards that had facts about endangered wildlife. The winner would be the one who saved the most animals.'

'Wonderful,' said Mrs Marshall. She turned to speak to the whole class. 'It sounds like Pippa's group is off to an excellent start. I hope the rest of you have all come up with something just as fabulous.'

The bell rang for lunch. I followed Meg,

Cici and Charlie out into the noisy playground. Most of our class drifted towards the big tree, chattering and laughing.

I sat down with the other girls and opened my lunch box.

'That was great thinking, Pippa,' said Cici, waving a carrot stick in the air. 'You saved us.'

I shook my head. 'It was Meg's idea.'

Meg glowed with pleasure. 'But you added in the detail.'

Olivia looked curiously at us. 'What did she do?'

Charlie looked around at all the girls. 'We were having a joke, making up silly ideas for the game. Then Mrs Marshall asked us what we were going to do. Quick as a flash, Pippa came up with a brilliant idea.'

Olivia swallowed a bite of her apple. 'So what *are* you doing for your project?'

'Oh, no,' said Cici. 'Good try. But we can't tell you. It's super-duper top-secret. Remember, the best project will be chosen to represent the school at the regional science competition on the mainland.'

'And Pippa's our lethal weapon,' said Charlie. 'Did you see how she blitzed the maths quiz?'

Olivia tossed her head. She didn't look at all pleased.

'So, Pippa,' she said. 'What school did you go to before?'

There was something about her tone that was not quite friendly. I hesitated for a moment. Even in the shade the air was sticky-hot.

'I went to Bromley House in Chelsea,' I said.

Thinking of my lovely, familiar school sent a wave of homesickness over me. I missed everything about it.

Olivia looked around at the other girls in a meaningful way. It made me feel unsure of myself all over again.

'That sounds posh,' said Olivia. 'Why did you leave there to come to Kira Island?'

That was something I definitely didn't want to discuss with Olivia and all these girls I hardly knew. It was still too raw.

Olivia raised her eyebrows at me. I had to say something.

'We . . . we had to move here,' I replied. I thought of what Meg had said about moving here for her mother's new job. 'My mum's renovating an old boatshed to make a cafe.'

Olivia laughed. 'Dad said someone had paid a ridiculous amount of money for that old tumbledown shack.'

Olivia smiled around at the girls. She looked delighted that she had succeeded in putting me firmly back in my place as the unwanted new girl.

I felt totally humiliated – and it didn't help that I thought Olivia might be right. Mum might have made a huge mistake and spent all our money on a ruin.

My first day at my new school was suddenly

not going so well, which is actually what I'd expected all along. I thought back to this morning when I'd taken ages getting dressed and eating breakfast. Mum had guessed that I was feeling sick with dread. She tried to convince me that everything would be sunshine and roses. But of course it wasn't! Why couldn't Mum take us back home to London where we belonged?

CHAPTER 3

THE BOATSHED

The bell rang to signal the end of school. Once dismissed, everyone rushed out the door without a backward glance.

I grabbed my bag and headed to the school gate. Mum was waiting for us inside the playground, by the front wall. She'd been working on the building site so she was wearing a pair of old jeans, a paint-spattered shirt, and her dark hair up in a messy knot on top of her head. I glanced around, hoping that no one would notice her looking like a hobo.

Bella was already there, telling Mum all about her day.

'I made six best new friends, Mumma,' said Bella. 'And my teacher, Miss Patel, is soooo nice.'

'*Six* best new friends?' repeated Mum with a fond smile. 'That's wonderful news, Bella-boo.'

Just then Olivia walked past, surrounded by a big group of girls and boys. She glanced at Mum, then smiled at me, but I didn't feel like it was a welcoming smile. She whispered something to Willow. I couldn't hear it but I was pretty sure I knew what she had said. Willow looked over and then quickly glanced away, her mouth twitching.

I flushed with embarrassment. Why on earth had Mum worn her oldest, grottiest work clothes to pick us up from school? I turned my back and pretended to be really interested in a line of ants scurrying across the playground.

Mum was oblivious. She kissed the top of my head. 'And how was your day, Pipkin?'

I pouted. Olivia's attitude at lunchtime still stung. I'd been worrying about it all afternoon. 'It was okay.'

Mum hugged me. 'You'll make friends, sweet pea. Just be your usual kind and funny self, and everyone will love you.'

It was easy for Mum to say everyone would love me. I thought of Olivia's comments. And what if she was right? What if Mum had been tricked into paying too much for a falling-down wreck? What if she'd dragged us halfway around the world just to ruin our lives?

'Hmmph,' I grumbled. 'I wish! But if we'd stayed in London I wouldn't have to make new friends.'

'Pipkin,' said Mum warningly. 'We've talked about this.'

Just then Harry came running up, his shirt hanging out and his dark hair standing on end. It seemed my brother had also had a pretty great day as he told Mum about the kids he'd met and the goals he'd kicked.

Mum led the way out of the gate. 'I thought we'd drop by the boatshed on our way home,' she said. 'The builders have been busy all day, so we're making good progress. I can't wait to show you.'

I rolled my eyes at Harry, but carefully so Mum didn't see.

We walked down towards the sheltered cove as Bella chatted all about her day. It was only a short way along a paved piazza, with quaint shops and tiny restaurants on each side. Then the vista opened to reveal a startling sweep of deep blue water. Colourful fishing boats bobbed up and down on their moorings. Seagulls squabbled over scraps along the sandy beach. People milled and strolled along the esplanade, enjoying the afternoon sunshine.

The boatshed, *our* boatshed, was built right on the shore of Kira Cove, connected to the esplanade by a short jetty. It was a big, two-storey timber building, with a round tower on the seaward side.

I know it might sound grand, but the boatshed was definitely a renovator's delight. The grey paint was dirty and peeling, and one of the double doors was leaning at a crazy angle. We could hear the sound of hammers banging and electric saws slicing through timber.

My heart sank as we walked inside the dark cavern of the shed. Mum had taken us to see it a few weeks ago, just before she bought it. I thought it was bad enough then, but it seemed even worse today. Builders bustled about wearing their clumpy workboots and tool-belts. Curls of timber shavings littered the floor along with piles of fine sawdust that made me sneeze. The smell of freshly cut timber mingled with the salt air and seaweed.

Mum gazed around with satisfaction. I'm not sure what she was so happy about. The place was a total mess.

'We've still got loads of work to do today,' said Mum. 'I thought you three might like to help. We need to carry all this rubbish outside.'

I groaned. 'I thought we were going home?'

Mum raised her eyebrows.

'Sure, Mum,' said Harry, putting down his schoolbag. 'Where do you want it?'

'In the back of the builder's ute, please. It's parked out the front.'

There was a huge pile of junk to one side. There was old rope, canvas, torn tarpaulins, cardboard boxes, crumbling newspapers, and even an old rowboat with a hole in it. I hated to think what might be living in that junk pile. Spiders? Cockroaches? Maybe even rats!

'But we can't,' I said, thinking of the perfect excuse to go home and draw. 'We'll get our new uniforms all dirty. We'd better just go back.'

'I thought of that,' Mum replied. She picked up a canvas tote bag that was leaning against the wall and passed it to me. 'I brought you some old clothes. You can get changed in the storeroom.'

Mum pulled on a pair of gardening gloves and picked up a load of rubbish. 'It won't take long if we all chip in.'

I pulled a torn T-shirt, a pair of my oldest shorts and a pair of canvas gloves from the bag, then passed it to Harry.

'Great,' I whispered to Harry once I thought Mum was out of earshot. 'I thought things couldn't get worse. But now we have to slave on this rotten old shack.'

Harry gave me a friendly shove towards the storeroom. 'Stop moaning, Pippa. Don't be such a princess. Mum needs all the help she can get.'

I turned my back on him and marched off to get changed. Princess indeed! My younger brother seemed to think he needed to be the man of the house now. The thought gave me those nasty butterflies all over again, and I tried to put thoughts of Dad out of my mind.

We carted stuff from the rubbish pile to the back of the builder's ute that was parked on the road by the esplanade. Bella skipped back and forth, carrying one or two items at a time. She was soon distracted by the tiny, pale soldier crabs that were rolling balls of sand on the beach.

Harry and I used an old washing basket to cart the garbage outside. We stooped and gathered junk, loaded the basket, lugged it outside, emptied it in the back of the truck, then went back inside to do it all over again. After an hour my arms and back ached. My throat was dry from dust and my nose itched. I was feeling tired and cross. This definitely wasn't how I wanted to spend my afternoon.

At last there was nothing left but the rotting rowboat.

'Help me carry this, sweet peas,' said Mum. 'It's quite heavy.'

'Quite heavy?' I asked. 'It feels like it's loaded with sandbags!'

The rowing boat wasn't going on the back of the truck. Mum had another plan for it, so we leaned it against the side of the wall outside. Mum had already stacked up a pile of old fishing nets and crab pots there.

We were just balancing the boat against the side of the shed when an old woman marched towards us. Despite the heat she was wearing a navy suit, a white shirt with a floppy bow at the throat, and big, round sunglasses. Her hair was set in perfect waves and she walked with a stick.

She scowled at us. 'Who's in charge here?'

The woman spoke with a slight foreign accent. Mum smiled at her. 'I'm Jenna Hamilton, and I'm the new owner. Can I help you?'

The old lady glowered even more. 'Your builders have been making noise for days. When are they going to stop? What are they doing?'

'The renovations should only take another

few weeks, Mrs . . . ?' said Mum, in a soothing voice.

'I'm Mrs Beecham, and I live across the road in the flat above the real estate office. And I tell you, the noise is intolerable. You need to stop, or I'll have to report you to the council.'

Bella chose this moment to come charging up, bellowing at the top of her voice. 'Mum! Mum! I found a shark egg!'

'That's lovely, Bella-boo, but show me in a minute,' said Mum.

Mrs Beecham glared at Bella and then Harry and me. 'And I won't tolerate children making a racket. I can't stand sassy children.' Her voice quavered on the last words as she stared at me. Bella's bottom lip trembled.

Harry and I exchanged secret glances. Mrs Beecham was too much. I almost expected her to wave her stick in Mum's face like a weapon.

Mum's smile was definitely wearing thin by now, and she was starting to look rather frazzled by our visitor.

'These are my children – Philippa, Henry and Isabella Hamilton,' she said. Mum was definitely stressed if she was using our full, formal names. That was reserved for near disasters or when she was really cross with us. 'They are generally well-behaved children so I doubt they will cause you any problems.'

Mrs Beecham huffed, looking at us as if she was convinced we were wild animals. 'They'd better be or I'll be letting you know. Good day.'

'Mrs Beecham?' pleaded Mum. But our new neighbour didn't stop to listen. Mrs Beecham stalked back past the builders, who were packing up the truck, without looking back.

What a horrible old woman! I thought. *Could this day possibly get any worse?*

CHAPTER 4

EXPLORING

Bella looked as though she might burst into tears. 'I want to go home.'

'We'll go home soon, Bella-boo,' said Mum soothingly. 'I just need to do a few things first.'

'Not to Mimi's,' insisted Bella, her voice wobbling. 'I want to go back to our *real* home. I want to go home with Dad.'

Mum looked stricken as she kissed Bella on top of her head. I thought quickly.

'Don't worry about Mrs Beecham, Bella,'

I whispered. 'She's just an old witch who likes scaring kids. Be brave and show her you're not frightened.'

Bella's eyes went round as limpets, then she gave a watery smile. Bella took her shark egg and wandered back onto the sand to search for more treasure.

'Well,' said Mum with a sigh. 'Problems with the neighbours already. That's all we need in a tiny place like this.'

One of the builders came over. He smiled at Mum. 'Don't worry about old Mrs B. She sounds gruff but she has a kind heart.'

I found that very difficult to believe. A heart of granite, more like it!

'Thanks, Jason,' said Mum. 'She was a bit intimidating.'

'She'll come round. But I do have a few things I need to talk to you about if you have a moment?'

'Of course,' said Mum. She turned to us.

'Why don't you two go and explore inside while I chat to Jason? You might find a lovely surprise if you look carefully.'

Mum and Jason began discussing plans and specifications and delayed timber deliveries, which all sounded pretty boring. Mum had her serious face on, so Harry and I were glad to escape.

The boatshed was now a big, shadowy space. It looked much bigger since we'd cleared out all the junk.

'I wonder what surprise Mum meant?' asked Harry, looking around as though he was a jungle adventurer discovering the wilds of Borneo.

'There's not that much to see,' I said. But my brother's enthusiasm was infectious, and we both started creeping around the boatshed.

Downstairs was a huge open space. The builders had started to create what Mum told us would be the kitchen and storeroom. Mum planned to make this level the cafe/bookshop/

arty homewares space. Right now, it just looked like a huge, empty shed with cracked, grey timber walls, and holes in the floor.

On the left-hand side was a set of stairs leading to the upper storey.

We raced up to the second level. Mum was planning for us to live up here eventually. Again it was a large open space, but with sloping ceilings like an attic. The builders would soon start framing up the walls to separate the area into different rooms.

Harry ran to the window on the beach side. He stared down at the builders chatting to Mum, the truck full of rubbish and Bella playing in the sand.

I wandered towards the water side. There was a small, grimy window looking out to sea.

Then I noticed something I hadn't seen before. There was another set of stairs, leading up to the ceiling. Actually, it was more like a narrow, rickety ladder.

'Harry!' I called. 'Look at this. It must lead up to the tower.'

I put my foot on the bottom rung and began to climb.

My head popped up through an opening in the ceiling and above the floor of the tower room. The air was full of choking dust that made me cough. I clambered up higher. The tower room was small and round and completely empty. I stepped onto the rickety floor, hoping it was safe. It felt like my foot might plunge through the floorboards again and I would tumble down through the ceiling to the level below.

The room had windows all around. Through the salt-smeared glass I could see the views back over the village of Kira Cove, to the mountains that reared olive-green and dark behind us. To the north the sweep of coral-white beach stretched away, and the wide, navy-blue sea. To the east was the tree-covered headland that protected the cove. Overhead was a huge dome of brilliant blue sky.

I lifted a rusty catch and pushed open a window. Fresh sea air blew in, puffing aside the dry dust and stuffy, stale heat. I could hear the sound of waves surging and pounding on the sandy shore. I breathed deeply, feeling my cranky mood being whipped away by the breeze. As I gazed out, a sudden movement caught my eye.

A glimpse of silvery-grey surging through the water. Then another and another. Was it a shark? Then I realised. It was a pod of dolphins swimming and cavorting in the bay below. I caught my breath in surprise. It was a magical sight.

'Harry, come here,' I cried. 'The view is amazing! I can see a whole pod of dolphins. There must be ten or twelve of them playing and diving.'

Harry clambered up the stairs behind me.

We stood in silence, watching the dolphins play. The water was so clear, you could see their silvery-grey bodies shimmering below.

One young dolphin jumped right out of the sea. It soared through the air and back down with a gigantic splash. I couldn't be certain, but it appeared to be looking up at us with an open, smiley mouth.

'Look at that cheeky one,' I said. 'He looks like he's laughing at us.'

The dolphin's smile was catching. Harry and I grinned back at the dolphins, watching them play until Mum called us down again. It was an amazing feeling to stand in that tower looking down over the cove, the village, the beach and back up to the mountains. It was like a miniature world. The world of Kira Island.

When Harry and I went down, Mum had said goodbye to the builders and was ready to lock up. Bella was on the beach, building a city out of twigs, shells, stones and sea-glass.

'Mum,' I said. 'Did you know that you can climb up to the tower? You can see the whole island from up there!'

'I thought that might cheer you up,' said Mum.

'We saw a pod of dolphins down in the cove,' added Harry. 'One of them was jumping and smiling at us.'

Mum beamed at us both. 'I wish I'd seen that. But it's a good omen, don't you think? Dolphins are super-lucky.'

I hoped so. My family needed all the luck we could get right now.

~~~~~~

My grandparents, Mimi and Papa, live in a gorgeous whitewashed stone cottage halfway along the ocean beach, surrounded by a big, lush tropical garden. Most of the houses in Kira Cove are painted the colour of vanilla ice-cream.

While the house is super-cute, it is tiny, so the four of us were sleeping in an old caravan in the backyard. There is a double bed at one end, which Mum and Bella share, then double bunks at the other end. I'm on the top bunk and Harry's down below. In the middle there's a tiny table and bench seats, a gas stove, a sink and a miniature fridge.

When we got back to the caravan, we all did our own activities until dinnertime. Bella and Mum were reading together, while Harry was practising his magic tricks in the garden. I was drawing the leaping dolphin in my notebook, trying to capture his cheeky smile.

Then Papa called us for dinner. We usually ate out on the patio under the frangipani tree. Mimi had made a big pot of her famous spa-ghetti bolognaise. When we were on holidays, I often helped Mimi cook, but with our first day at school and working at the boatshed and the excitement of the dolphins, the day had whizzed past.

Papa ladled sauce onto our pasta and Mimi handed the plates around. We told them all about our first day at school while we slurped up the long, stringy spaghetti.

'I found a shark egg washed up on the beach, with a tiny baby shark inside,' said Bella. 'Mum said I can take it to school for show-and-tell tomorrow. And there was a wicked witch that came to the boatshed today.'

'A wicked witch?' asked Mimi with a repressed smile.

'We met one of our new neighbours,' said Mum. 'Mrs Beecham, who hates builders and hates noise.'

'And hates kids,' I added. 'Careful, Bella. She might take you for a ride on her broomstick.'

Mimi put her hand over mine. 'Mrs Beecham doesn't hate anyone. She's just lonely and in pain with her arthritis.'

I felt a tiny flicker of remorse.

Papa turned to Mum. 'And how was your day? Did the builders get much done?'

Mum looked worried for a moment. 'Oh, yes. It seems to be going okay, and the kids helped me clean out all the rubbish from the bottom level, so we can get a good sense of the space now.'

'So do you think it will be ready in time for the planned opening celebration?' asked Mimi. Mum wanted to throw a party to officially launch the cafe when it was finished.

'I hope so,' said Mum. 'The books are all ordered and the furniture's on its way. But Jason, the builder, warned me that deliveries to the island can sometimes be unreliable. So let's hope nothing else gets delayed.'

'Else?' asked Mimi. 'Has something gone wrong already?'

Mum sighed. 'We're waiting on a big delivery of timber that was meant to arrive a few days ago, but apparently it went to the wrong island.'

'How could it go to the wrong island?' I asked. 'That's crazy.'

51

'It was loaded on the wrong ferry, unloaded on the other end and is still sitting there. Jason said it will probably turn up eventually.'

Papa laughed. 'That's one of the charming things about Kira. Island time runs differently to the rest of the busy world.'

'But I promised the bank we'd open in three weeks,' said Mum. 'We need to start earning money as soon as possible.'

Money had been very tight in our family since we left London. Mum was pinning all her hopes on the cafe being a huge success.

Mimi raised her glass in a toast. 'Don't worry, darling. Things will work out.'

I just hoped she was right. It didn't look very promising to me at the moment.

CHAPTER 5

DANCE WITH MISS DEMI

The next few days at school were better, as I settled into the routine and started to remember faces and names. That was until the last class on Thursday, which was dance with Miss Demi. Miss Demi was a young teacher in a black singlet and leggings who was brimming with energy and enthusiasm.

Back home I enjoyed dancing but I must confess I'd never been the best at it. I always struggled to remember the steps and my rhythm was way off. When I was learning the piano in London, I was hopeless at it (although my music teacher told Mum a little practice would help). So you can imagine how hard it was for me in Miss Demi's class, where all the other kids had been learning the routine for weeks already. It was truly awful!

I felt like a baby elephant as I tried to pick up the moves. I was stretching to the sky while everyone else was sweeping to the ground, or I was jumping left, while everyone else was hopping right.

Miss Demi had me behind Olivia, copying her. But Olivia seemed so graceful and polished that it just made me feel more hopeless.

The worst part was when I jumped the wrong way and crashed right into the boy next to me. My outstretched arm smashed into the poor boy's nose.

'Oowww,' he cried, tears of pain filling his eyes as he clutched his nose. Everyone stopped dancing and turned to look. What a disaster!

'Oh, I'm so sorry,' I cried, blushing the colour of a Kira Island sunset.

'Alex, are you okay?' asked Olivia, rushing over to help him.

Alex garbled a muffled response. Olivia turned to the teacher. 'Miss Demi, should I take Alex to see the nurse? He might have broken his nose.'

Miss Demi came over, looking worried. She checked Alex's nose. It was bright red and swollen. 'Good idea, Olivia. Thank you – that's very kind.'

Olivia and Alex headed out of the hall.

'Come on, 5M,' said Miss Demi. 'Let's get back to work. Pippa, perhaps you should just sit and watch for a while. I'm sure you'll pick it up soon.'

I wanted to shrink inside myself like a turtle. I sat up the back on my own, watching and trying to memorise the choreography.

After school, we planned to go to Meg's to work on our science project. But first I had to meet Bella and Harry and walk them to the boatshed.

Mum had decided that instead of picking us up as she had always done in London, she wanted me to walk my brother and sister home. She said it would be good for me to have some extra responsibility now that she had so much to do at the building site. Of course, because Mum wasn't there it took ages to chase up Bella and herd her out of the playground. She was having too much fun playing with all her new friends on the monkey bars.

By the time I'd extracted Bella, Harry had disappeared. It was very frustrating. I was a bit annoyed with Mum. Really, it would have been so much easier if she'd come by the school.

In the end we all walked down to the beach together – Harry, Bella, Charlie, Meg, Cici and me. The boatshed was a busy, noisy scene of builders bustling around sawing and hammering. I paused outside, hoping the girls would want to wait for me there.

'I won't be long,' I said. 'I'll just tell Mum where I'm going.'

'No rush,' said Meg. 'What are they building?'

'In London, Mum worked as a stockbroker,' I said. 'But there are no jobs like that here on Kira Island. So Mum has this crazy plan of turning the shed into a cafe and bookshop.'

'That sounds great,' said Charlie.

'Maybe,' I said gloomily. 'But the place is a wreck.'

The girls followed me inside and stared around. Mum was standing at a trestle table, poring over plans and lists. Behind her, the builders had partially erected some walls and a counter.

'Hello, girls,' said Mum. 'Have you come to help with the sanding?'

I introduced the girls to Mum and, before I knew it, Mum was giving them the guided tour, pointing out where everything would be. She did make it sound promising.

'The cafe will be like a gorgeous living room, with comfy sofas, squashy cushions, bookshelves and buckets of fresh flowers,' said Mum, waving her hand around like a magic wand. 'Then outside on the jetty, we'll have pretty tables and chairs in the sunshine so customers can enjoy the views.'

'It's just like one of those TV shows,' said Cici. Her brown eyes sparkled with enthusiasm. 'You know, where they take a ramshackle old building, and turn it into an amazingly stylish home.'

'Won't it be great to have a cafe so close to school?' said Charlie. 'We could meet here in the afternoon. Everyone will love having somewhere to go.'

'Especially a cafe with yummy cupcakes and mango smoothies,' added Cici.

'I think we can manage that, can't we, Pipkin?' said Mum.

Charlie, Meg and Cici beamed at me.

'I guess so,' I said. For the first time since we'd left London, weeks ago, I felt a flicker of excitement. Perhaps their enthusiasm was contagious.

Mum wanted me to drop some mail into the postbox, so the girls and I waited out the front while Mum finished getting organised. Our boatshed was built on a wooden pier that jutted above the sandy beach and over the water. An esplanade ran alongside the beach in both directions with a wide strip of lawn lined with palm trees.

The paved pathway was busy with kids riding bikes, parents pushing prams and people walking their dogs. I looked longingly at all the dogs, imagining which kind I'd love to have. A golden retriever with a lolling tongue, a cute spotted beagle, a shaggy terrier or a big, goofy labrador? In London, I'd always loved fussing over the dogs being walked in Battersea Park near our home. But even though I'd begged and begged to have our own dog, Mum said that our terrace courtyard was way too tiny.

A group of boys from our class cruised past on their skateboards. They waved at us. I suddenly realised that one of them was Alex, the boy I'd smashed in the face during dance class. The girls called out hello.

I felt my cheeks reddening and quickly glanced out to sea, remembering the humiliation of dance with Miss Demi.

'Poor Alex,' said Charlie. 'His nose still looks a bit puffy.'

'At least it wasn't really broken,' said Meg. 'Just a bit swollen.'

I winced. 'Don't remind me. I thought I'd die of embarrassment.'

'It was pretty funny,' said Cici, with a grin. She did a little impersonation of me awkwardly dancing, pretending to knock Meg over.

Meg looked at me with understanding. 'It's hard to learn a new dance when everyone else knows it.'

Charlie flicked her long hair over her shoulder. 'We should practise with you. It's pretty easy once you get the hang of it.'

'I don't even recognise the song,' I confessed.

'It's one of our favourites,' said Cici. 'It's called "Love and Laughter", by Ruby Starr. She's a famous singer who went to our school when she was younger.'

'I adore her music,' said Charlie. 'I can play nearly all Ruby's songs on the guitar.' Charlie began to sing the song, playing an invisible guitar. She had a lovely voice.

'Dance positions,' urged Cici.

Charlie, Cici and Meg crouched down on the lawn, their heads curled to their chests.

'And one, two, three, four ... and up,' instructed Cici.

The three girls leapt to their feet. Cici called out the directions as they danced. 'And step, one, two, three and twist ...' Charlie kept singing the words. I began to copy them, concentrating hard to memorise the steps. It went really well for the first two minutes.

We all joined in singing the song, dancing on the grass in the hot summer sunshine. Then, of course, I miscalculated and jumped to my right as the girls jumped to their left. Meg, Charlie and I ended up in a tumble of arms and legs on the ground, howling with laughter.

'Well, that didn't go so well,' joked Cici, flopping down on the ground beside us. 'More like baby hippos than graceful gazelles.'

I sat up, my cheeks aching with merriment.

'What on earth is this ruckus?' boomed a familiar voice. It was Mrs Beecham, our crotchety new neighbour, glaring at me.

'We . . . we were just laughing,' I tried to explain. A giggle bubbled up, threatening to burst free. 'I mean, we were singing and then we fell over . . . and . . .'

'Don't you be sassy with me, Philippa Hamilton,' snapped Mrs Beecham, leaning on her stick. 'I've already told your mother that I won't tolerate rambunctious children or deafening builders destroying the peace of my neighbourhood. It's a disgrace.'

I remembered Mrs Beecham's threat to report Mum to the council. That would be a huge worry that Mum didn't need right now. I felt crushed.

'Sorry, Mrs Beecham,' I mumbled. 'We were practising something for school.'

'Where's your mother?' Mrs Beecham demanded. 'I need a word with her.'

The old lady stormed off in the direction of the boatshed, huffing and puffing her annoyance.

'What was her problem?' asked Meg, raising an eyebrow.

'She just hates kids,' I replied. 'Especially noisy kids.'

'You mean *rambunctious* kids?' said Cici with a grin.

'Or is it *sassy* kids she hates most?' suggested Charlie.

We all giggled some more.

A few minutes later, Mum escorted Mrs Beecham back out the door. She looked harried as she gave me the mail to post on the way to Meg's. Before we could cause any more ruckus, the four of us headed off.

CHAPTER 6

DOLPHIN TALK

Meg's yacht was about five minutes away, moored off a jetty in the bay. The yacht was sleek and white, with a timber deck, a tall mast and the sails furled along the boom. Some washing flapped on a line strung across the stern. We scrambled aboard across a narrow plank and onto the bow of the yacht.

Further back was the cockpit, set low into the deck. It had narrow benches along each side and the large steering wheel at the back. A door was open, leading down a ladder into the main cabin.

'Hi, Mum, are you home?' called Meg.

'Down below,' answered a voice.

We all followed Meg down into the cabin. Meg's mum was sitting at the small dining table working on her laptop. She looked up with a welcoming smile.

'Mum, this is Pippa Hamilton,' said Meg. 'She started at school with us last week. Pippa, this is my mum, Mariana.'

We all said hello.

A grey tabby cat came and wound his way around Meg's legs, meowing loudly. She picked him up and gave him a rub on the head.

'This is our ship's cat, Neptune,' said Meg. 'He visits the trawlers every morning to beg for a fishy treat. Everyone who works on the harbour knows him.'

Meg showed us around. It reminded me a bit of our caravan, with a narrow cabin for Meg's parents in the front, a tiny kitchen and dining table in the middle and two tiny beds at the back, tucked one on either side of the steps under the deck. Next to the kitchen was a bank of complicated-looking machinery with dials, screens and lights. Above it was a shelf laden with cameras, binoculars and cables.

'What's all this for?' I asked.

'It's the equipment for Mum's research,' replied Meg. She picked up a flat, round microphone with a long cable. 'Mum swims in the ocean with wild dolphins, using hydrophones like this and underwater video cameras to record their different noises.'

Mariana looked up, her face alight with enthusiasm. 'There are so many ways that dolphins communicate. They squeak, click and whistle, and use body language. It's fascinating.'

'Did you know that every dolphin has an individual whistle, which is like a name?' Meg asked me. 'If you record that noise and play it back, the dolphin responds, just like you would if I called out Pippa.'

'Wow,' I said. 'So you can actually speak with the dolphins.'

Mariana nodded. 'On a simple level for now, but perhaps in years to come we might be able to truly communicate.'

Meg looked proud. 'The dolphins even have a special whistle for Mum. They have a game they like to play where they steal a rope from us and toss it back and forth from snout to snout, like they're playing catch.'

'That's my dog Muffin's favourite game too,' said Cici, with a grin. 'Only Meg, the Wildlife Whisperer, would have pet dolphins that play catch.'

Charlie and I giggled. I imagined a dolphin coming to Meg's whistle and wagging its tail.

'They're not pets,' said Meg, looking serious. 'They're wild creatures. We're really careful not to feed the dolphins or handle them unnecessarily.'

'I'd love to play with wild dolphins,' Charlie said, wistfully.

'One day I'll take you girls out with me on a research trip,' Mariana promised.

'That would be amazing,' I said. I looked around the yacht with a thrill of excitement. Meg certainly had an interesting life.

'Speaking of studying animals,' said Meg, 'perhaps we should go and do some research of our own.'

The four of us went back up and sat on the benches in the cockpit. Meg brought the laptop with her so we could look up fun facts for our game.

'Could you toss me a cushion, please, Meg?' asked Cici. Meg opened a hatch under the bench seat and passed out four navy cushions.

'Everything is so tidy on your yacht,' I said. 'Our place seems to get messy so fast.'

'We've lived on a yacht for years now, so it's just easier if everyone keeps it tidy,' said Meg. 'Besides, there's not much storage space so we don't actually have much stuff.'

I couldn't imagine living on a yacht permanently. One of the things I was missing most about our old house back in London was having my own room. Normally I got on really well with my brother and sister, but without my safe haven to escape to, they were really starting to drive me crazy.

'I wish we had a not-much-stuff rule at home,' said Charlie. 'With five kids in the house, it's a bit chaotic.'

'And *super*-noisy!' said Cici.

'Five kids?' I asked. 'Wow, that's a big family.'

'It wasn't always so big,' said Charlie. 'For ages it was just Mum, my sister Sophia, and me. Now I have two stepbrothers, Oscar and Seb, and my half-sister, Daisy. She's only six.'

'That must have been hard to get used to,' I said.

'I thought it would be horrible but it's actually really fun,' said Charlie. 'There's always someone to talk to or play with. And it's nice to see Mum so happy. My stepdad, Dave, is really great.'

For a moment I wondered what it would be like to have a stepdad. I pushed the thought away. I just wished I had my own dad back.

I turned to Cici. 'And what about your family?'

'We're just a totally *normal* family,' said Cici. 'I have an older brother called Will, who is twelve and in the same class as Jack. My mum's a fashion designer, so she travels all over the world for the international shows. That's how she met my dad at Hong Kong Fashion Week. Mum has her own label and creates the most gorgeous clothes. My dad is a pastry chef and makes the best cakes in the world.'

'That doesn't sound normal to me,' I replied. 'Your parents sound incredible.'

I was curious to learn more about these three girls. Would Meg's mum really take us out sailing to meet the dolphins? What was Charlie's big mixed family like? And what would it be like to have a dad who made the best cakes in the world? I was suddenly very glad that Mrs Marshall had put me in their science group.

~~~~~~~

The yacht rocked gently as we worked on our project.

We sat around the cockpit and pored over the computer, looking up information on endangered African animals like the elephant, lion, cheetah, gorilla and rhinoceros. It made me sad to think that these beautiful animals were in danger.

'Did you know that tens of thousands of African elephants are killed each year for their ivory tusks?' asked Meg. Her brown eyes sparked with anger.

We looked at the screen, where there were photos of beautiful elephants and their calves, piles of ivory tusks, then a pile of bangles and pendants.

'That's awful,' said Charlie.

'Who would wear that jewellery, knowing that elephants were killed to make it?' I asked.

'Selfish, horrible people,' said Cici.

'That's why we have to make a really good game,' said Meg, looking at us all intently. 'Mum says most people don't realise the implications of their actions. If they knew that by using plastic shopping bags, they might be responsible for killing turtles or dolphins, then they wouldn't do it.'

Cici put her hand on Meg's arm and smiled affectionately. 'Meg has her Wildlife Warrior face on.'

'So you mean our game could teach kids about animals and the danger they're in?' I asked. 'Which might help save them?'

It seemed unlikely that four kids could do anything to help save the animals. The problem seemed too big.

Meg nodded. 'If lots of kids play our game they'd learn about which animals are in danger and what we can do to stop it.'

'*Especially* if we win the school competition and go to the regional science competition,' said Cici, waggling her eyebrows like an evil scientist.

'Right,' said Charlie. 'We'd better get started then. How is this game going to work?'

'First we need to draw a game plan on cardboard for the pieces to move around with traps and challenges,' said Meg.

'Lots of people will probably do that,' said Cici. 'Ours has to be really *awesome*.'

'Well, why don't we make a 3D board out of papier-mâché?' I said. 'We could have mountains and plains and rainforest to represent the different habitats, and use toy animals.'

I immediately thought of Bella's collection of plastic jungle animals that were tucked away in a shoebox at the bottom of the cupboard.

She never played with them anymore and our game would *definitely* be a much better use for them.

'Great idea,' said Charlie. 'I'll raid our games cupboard at home for dice and something we can use for players to move around the board.'

I wrote down a list of animals to include:

10 MOST ENDANGERED ANIMALS IN AFRICA

1. Addax
2. Ethiopian wolf
3. Mountain gorilla
4. Pygmy hippopotamus
5. African wild dog
6. Black rhinoceros
7. African cheetah
8. African lion
9. African penguin
10. African elephant

'Who'd have thought the most endangered animal in Africa was an addax?' I said, as I marked it down in my best handwriting.

'I've never even heard of an addax,' said Cici.

'It's a kind of white antelope,' said Meg, checking on the screen. 'There are only about two hundred left in the world.'

'So why are there so few left?' asked Charlie.

'People, of course,' said Meg fiercely. 'Addax are hunted and their natural habitat is taken over by farming.'

We spent the next hour brainstorming good ideas for our game. I wrote out a list of jobs for everyone to work on at home.

CHARLIE

- Research fun facts on pygmy hippopotamuses and African penguins.
- Find player pieces and dice.
- Design artwork for cards.

CICI

- Research mountain gorillas, Ethiopian wolves and African wild dogs.
- Write rule book.
- Make challenge cards.

MEG

- Research addaxes, black rhinos and cheetahs.
- Research strategies to save animals.
- Make fact cards on animals.

PIPPA

- Research African elephants and lions.
- Design awesome 3D board.
- Check with builders for material we can recycle for board, e.g. timber, paint, plywood.
- Find Bella's jungle animals.

That night, as I snuggled into my bunk bed, Mum came to kiss me goodnight. She stroked my forehead.

'Our neighbour, Mrs Beecham, was a little upset this afternoon,' said Mum.

I felt worried. What awful things had Mrs Beecham said to Mum?

'She complained about the building noise again,' continued Mum. 'But she also said you and your friends were being a bit wild today?'

So I told her how we had been singing and laughing as we practised the dance. I felt guilty that we'd upset Mrs Beecham again.

'I'm sorry, Mum,' I said. 'We didn't mean to be noisy. We were just having fun, but when I tried to explain, Mrs Beecham told me not to be sassy.'

Mum hugged me close. 'Don't you worry about Mrs Beecham. She was brought up in a time when children, especially girls, were meant to be seen and not heard. But that's not what I want for you.'

'What do you mean?' I asked.

'Well, Mrs Beecham is really paying you a compliment, even if she didn't mean to,' Mum said. 'Sassy means someone who is strong, smart, brave and bold, which is exactly what I hope you'll be all through your life.'

I nodded, thinking about what Mum had said. Sassy sounded good when you put it like that.

'Just remember that Mrs Beecham is old and crotchety because she's lonely and in pain, so try to be kind to her,' said Mum.

Be kind to Mrs Beecham, who hates kids? I thought. Not likely. Her gibe about being sassy still stung.

I wasn't sure that Mum was right so I looked it up on our computer the next morning. The online definition said, **'Sassy /sasi/ – lively, bold, and full of spirit'**, although another definition did list it as rude and disrespectful, which is probably more what Mrs Beecham had in mind.

CHAPTER 7

EAVESDROPPING

On Friday we only had lessons in the morning. We had free reading, a spelling test and some class time to discuss our science projects. Then we had to mark all our homework for the week.

Mrs Marshall stopped by my desk to check my homework. She nodded her approval.

'Excellent work, Pippa,' she said. 'You're really settling in well. I think you are going to be one of my star students.'

Olivia glanced at me and frowned.

I glowed with pleasure. To be honest, the work we had done at Bromley House was a little ahead of what we were doing here, so I found the schoolwork quite easy. But it was nice to be thought of as clever.

The bell went for lunchtime. On Friday afternoons all the students had sport. At home at my old school, we played hockey or tennis (I was truly terrible at tennis), and I'd even spent a year competing on the fencing team.

But here at Kira Cove School, during summer the students had a choice of swimming, surfing, sailing or kayaking. Charlie said they played sports like football and netball during the winter when it was cooler.

Thankfully, Mrs Marshall allocated me to the kayaking group with Charlie, Meg and Cici. I'd never done it before but it sounded easier than surfing or sailing, and I was glad to be doing it with the other girls.

Lunchtime was a flurry of activity as

everyone ate their lunch quickly, then got ready. We changed into our swimming costumes and rash vests, and put on sunscreen and hats. The kids chattered with excitement. Then we all walked in a long double line down to the beach.

Olivia was walking in front of me. She turned around and looked at me.

'Nice swimming costume,' she said, but I could tell by her tone that she really meant the opposite. My swimming costume was the one I'd worn at my old school and was boring navy-blue. Suddenly I realised all the other girls were wearing brightly coloured costumes of lolly-pink, orange, aqua and pastel-green.

I wanted to explain that we hadn't had the time or money to buy a new swimming costume since we'd arrived. Instead I just blushed and looked awkward and gabbled something about getting a new one soon. Olivia always seemed to make me feel clumsy.

Olivia just turned away and started talking to Sienna about gymnastics class.

Down at the marina we met our instructors and split into groups. The kayakers put on life jackets and paired up. I was with Charlie, and Cici and Meg were together. Then we dragged our bright-orange plastic kayaks down into the water and climbed in.

I wobbled like crazy and had to sit down fast, clinging onto the sides. The kayak rocked violently and Charlie steadied it with both hands. She pushed the kayak out further, then leapt in behind me.

'Okay, paddle,' said Charlie. 'It won't take long to get the hang of it.'

That was easy for Charlie to say. We each had a double-sided paddle, which we dipped into the water one side after the other. I tried to copy what Meg and Cici were doing in the other kayak. But I kept paddling too hard so I was out of time with Charlie. This swung the nose around so we veered in a circle. Then I accidentally reached too far back and whacked Charlie's paddle with mine.

'Ouch,' she cried. I dropped the paddle in surprise.

'Sorry,' I said as my paddle floated away out of reach.

Charlie laughed. 'At least you didn't get my head, although it was pretty close!'

Meg and Cici giggled as they watched my clumsy attempts to reach for the paddle, nearly capsizing our kayak in the process. They zipped over and rescued my escaping paddle, handing it back to me.

'Let's try again,' said Charlie. 'Sit up straighter and I'll call the stroke so we synchronise better.'

Instead of going in a direct line, we kept zigzagging back and forth until I gradually got into a better rhythm. Then I began to relax and look about us.

It was another perfect Kira Island day –

brilliant with sunshine, a slight cooling breeze, and the sparkling sapphire-blue cove.

We paddled out through the colourful boats and into the open water to join the other kids. The instructor had briefed us to slowly paddle out and around a course of floating buoys, then back to the marina. But the kids had other ideas!

'Race you guys,' called a boy from the kayak next to us. I realised it was Alex, and his friend Rory.

'Okay,' agreed Charlie. 'Ready, set, go!'

'But . . .' I tried to object, not sure that my brand-new paddling skills were up to a race, but the others were already off. Charlie started paddling behind me and I just had to do my best to keep up with her.

A group of other kayaks was paddling for the first buoy. There were six teams – Charlie and me, Alex and Rory, Cici and Meg, Sam and Joey, Olivia and Sienna, Hamish and Luke.

We paddled like crazy but Charlie and I had no chance since it was my very first time in a kayak. We came in a very slow last!

Luckily, Charlie didn't seem to mind. Meg and Cici were really good and came in equal first with Sam and Joey. The boys celebrated by bombing off their kayak into the water and splashing everyone.

Sam and Joey disappeared underwater. I was a bit worried about them because we were so far offshore and I wondered what might be down in the deep. Sharks? Stingrays? Or a giant octopus? I peered down into the shadowy depths.

Suddenly our kayak lurched. I nearly dropped my paddle again.

'What was that?' I asked Charlie.

Charlie gripped onto the side of the kayak. 'A humpback whale or two?' It took me a moment to realise she was joking.

The kayak lurched again and Charlie and I were tossed out of the boat and into the water.

I spluttered to the surface, thrashing my arms, my life jacket keeping me afloat. Of course, it was Sam and Joey who had overturned our kayak. They resurfaced shouting with laughter and lithely climbed back into their kayak.

I found it a lot harder. I slipped and slithered, splashing back into the sea every time. My arms felt weak from the unusual exercise and I didn't have the strength to pull myself up. Finally, Charlie had to haul me in, nearly capsizing the kayak again. The other kids chuckled at my clumsy rescue, but not in a nasty way. Only Olivia looked delighted at my predicament.

'Last one back to shore is a stinky slug,' yelled Joey. He and Sam raced off, closely followed by the other teams.

'I can't race again,' I cried, slumping over my paddle. 'My arms are like jelly!'

'That's okay,' said Charlie, lying back on the stern and closing her eyes. 'Let's float for a bit.'

Cici and Meg drifted along beside us, waiting

for me to recover. We bobbed around out on the sea, chatting about our plans for the weekend, then slowly paddled back towards shore. Suddenly Charlie whispered to me.

'Stop. Look.'

I lifted my paddle out of the water and gazed around. A sleek silver-grey head broke the surface. Then another and another. Our two kayaks were drifting in the middle of a pod of dolphins. The dolphins surged and swam around us, peeking at us curiously.

'Aren't they amazing?' I said, my voice hushed with wonder.

'Meg's mum says that dolphins are the most intelligent animals on the planet after humans,' said Charlie.

'This is the pod of bottlenose dolphins that Mum's studying,' said Meg, from the next kayak. 'That's my favourite, Artemis. I can tell her by that notch in her dorsal fin.'

Meg pointed out a dolphin who was

swimming closer to us, with a distinctive scar on her fin.

'She has a boy calf called Jupiter,' explained Meg, pointing to a smaller dolphin beside her. 'He's really playful.'

As if to prove her right, Jupiter jumped straight out of the water and grinned at us. I wondered if he was the cheeky boy I'd seen from the boatshed tower.

The four of us floated on our kayaks, watching. Artemis swam right up to us on her side, and peered at us with one eye, as if she was just as fascinated by us as we were with her.

'She's checking us out,' said Cici.

'Artemis likes humans,' said Meg, putting her hand in the water. 'She was orphaned as a baby and the marine biologists at Marine Animal Rescue saved her life. She came in every evening to the beach and they fed her fish until she was old enough to fend for herself. Now she comes to visit us quite often off the back of the yacht.'

Artemis swam closer and bumped Meg's hand with her snout. A strand of seaweed floated by. Meg grabbed it and tossed it to Artemis. Artemis took the seaweed and raced away with it in her mouth. Jupiter gave chase. Artemis dived deep, then passed the weed to Jupiter, who tossed it back. Then Artemis swam back and presented the seaweed to Meg.

'Wow,' I said. 'Meg, you *are* a dolphin whisperer!'

Meg beamed with pleasure. 'When I was younger I played with more dolphins than other kids. I really do wish I could talk to them.'

The dolphins swam around us for a while, then, as if by some secret signal, they sank beneath the waves and disappeared. The four of us looked at each other, speechless with exhilaration. It was one of the most beautiful things I'd ever seen. And it was so special to share it with these three girls who were becoming my friends. I paddled back to shore in a cloud of happiness.

We were the last two crews back to shore. In pairs, we carried the kayaks up the beach, hosed them off and stowed them in the storage shed. I raced back to get the paddles and started hosing them off beside the shed.

I heard a group of the kids chatting and laughing around the corner. Suddenly I recognised a voice. It was Olivia.

'Did you see Philippa?' she asked. 'She was *hopeless*. It was pretty funny watching her trying to get back in the kayak.'

I shrank back against the wall. I didn't want to hear what they were saying, but I couldn't bring myself to walk away.

'I guess Pippa hasn't done much kayaking before,' replied a boy's voice. I think it was Joey. 'She did well for her first try.'

'She thinks she's so cool,' said Olivia. I wasn't

imagining it. Her tone had definitely turned nasty. 'With her posh accent, and bragging about her swanky London school. It's like she's looking down her nose at us all.'

'Pippa seems all right,' said another boy. It might have been Alex.

'But she nearly broke your nose,' Olivia said. 'She was just trying to show off.'

It *was* Alex! I cringed. I couldn't believe Olivia was talking about me like that behind my back.

The voices moved off, so I skulked back to put the paddles away. We all changed into dry clothes and milled around outside, waiting for Mrs Marshall to mark the roll. Most people had changed into casual clothes rather than their school uniforms.

While the others chattered about the dolphins and the race, I kicked a stone along the footpath, feeling angry and upset and lonely all at once.

When the roll was marked, everyone was allowed to go home. Olivia stopped beside us and smiled winningly.

'Bye, girls. See you tomorrow at three o'clock.' She waved and wandered off.

'See you tomorrow,' mumbled Charlie and Cici, looking embarrassed.

Tomorrow? What's happening on Saturday? I thought. But I had a terrible feeling that Olivia had organised something and not invited me.

Meg confirmed it, looking at me apologetically. 'Olivia's organised a pool party at her house tomorrow afternoon, and invited a few kids from our class.'

'She sort of organised it before, when she didn't really know you,' Cici explained.

'I thought she might have invited you today,' added Charlie. 'I'm sure her mum wouldn't mind if you came along. I could ring her?'

'No.' I could still hear Olivia's scornful voice in my head. Clearly Olivia didn't like me and

I wasn't going to go where I wasn't wanted. 'Thanks all the same but I'm helping Mum tomorrow.'

The girls looked relieved.

'Well, would you all like to come back to my house this afternoon?' suggested Cici. 'I thought we could bake some chocolate brownies for afternoon tea and watch a movie.'

Charlie and Meg quickly agreed. I thought about it for a moment but I didn't really feel like it now. Cici was probably only asking to make up for Olivia leaving me out.

'No, I can't. I have to pick up Harry and Bella from school. Besides, Mum will have some job she needs me to do at the boatshed.'

'Are you sure?' asked Cici. 'You could come by a bit later.'

'It will be fun,' said Charlie.

I stubbornly shook my head.

So that's how I came to spend my whole weekend sanding walls and sweeping floors at the boatshed. As you can imagine, it was miserable.

CHAPTER 8

THE EVIL SEA WITCH

We worked all day Sunday in the boatshed and, as far as I could see, we hadn't made much difference. By three o'clock we were sticky and sweaty and grubby. And, I must admit, pretty grumpy.

Mum wiped her hand across her forehead and gave us all a tired smile. 'Let's pack up and go home. We've done enough for today.'

'Can we go for a swim on the way, Mumma?' asked Bella.

'Sure, Bella-boo,' said Mum. 'It'll be good to wash off all this grime.'

We changed into our swimming costumes and threw our clothes on over the top, then Bella and Harry raced outside. I picked up my backpack and towel.

'Could you grab the keys for me, please, Pipkin?' called Mum from the front door. 'I think I left them on the trestle table.'

The boatshed keys were on the table next to Mum's ideas album. Mum had a big folder that was jammed with photographs, magazine clippings and swatches of material in every hue of blue and green. The photographs were of beautifully styled homewares and interiors. Comfy armchairs with fluffy cushions, massed bowls of flowers, candles and lanterns, mounds of fruit and long timber tables heaped with food.

Next to the album was a pile of bills. Invoices from builders, the plumber, electrician, timber merchant and furniture suppliers; for the coffee machine, kitchen equipment, crockery, books and hardware. I didn't mean to snoop, but I couldn't help but see a fragment of the letter that was half-hidden under the pile. '... *writing to inform you that your bank account is overdrawn by $23,542.53. Please deposit money as soon as possible ...*'

I picked up the keys and looked around. Despite all the work, it was still a big, dusty, dilapidated shed. And Mum had promised the bank it would be open for business in two weeks. It seemed hopeless.

'Come on, Pipkin,' called Mum. 'Don't look so glum. You'll feel better after a swim.'

Mum locked up the boatshed and we started walking up the esplanade.

Bella skipped along, chattering non-stop about her new friends. Harry was kicking his soccer ball along the footpath.

Suddenly I noticed a group of girls riding skateboards towards us. Then I realised it was Cici, Charlie, Meg and *Olivia*. Cici had a small brown dog on a lead running along beside her. She looked far more stylish out of school uniform – in a gorgeous black beach dress with an embroidered border of red, blue and yellow around the skirt.

'Hey, Pippa,' called Charlie, waving madly. She was wearing a cream crocheted boho top with a daisy print skirt and sandals. A collection of silver bangles jangled on her wrist. Her hair was out of its plait and floating down her back in curly, golden waves.

'Hi,' I replied, feeling awkward. I was suddenly super-super-conscious of my grubby shorts, torn T-shirt and greasy hair pulled back in a ponytail.

So too was Olivia, judging by the way she looked us up and down. Mum, Harry and Bella all looked equally dishevelled but they seemed completely oblivious to her disdainful gaze.

Olivia was cool and pretty in denim shorts and a floral tank top. Only Meg was more casual, wearing a loose green T-shirt and shorts with runners.

I leant down and stroked the little dog. 'She's adorable. Is she yours, Cici?'

'Yes. This is Muffin,' said Cici, hopping off her skateboard. 'She's a puggle – half pug, half beagle – and super-curious.'

Muffin grinned up at me, her tongue lolling out and her tail wagging madly. She had a curled-up tail and a wrinkled face that made her look worried.

'I'd love to have a dog,' I said, cuddling Muffin. 'Mum's been promising us one for ages. We couldn't have one in London. At home we used to have two goldfish, Captain Jack and Angelique, but we had to leave them behind.'

Something else we had to leave behind. I carefully avoided looking at Mum. Bella had been lobbying for a new pet, preferably a dinosaur, but I wasn't sure anymore. For years I'd pestered Mum to let us get a dog in London, but I'd stopped asking. If we got a new pet now it would mean we were definitely staying here on Kira Island. And that was the last thing I wanted.

'That must have been hard,' said Meg.

'It was sad,' I said. 'But I gave them to my friend Miranda, and she promised to look after them.'

'Goldfish are pretty boring pets,' said Olivia. 'I used to have fish but now I have four guinea pigs.'

Thanks, Olivia!

'We're just going for a swim. Do you want to come with us?' said Charlie, changing the subject.

I didn't. Not with Olivia there. I'd started to think of Charlie, Cici, Meg and I as a foursome. Seeing them skateboarding with Olivia made me feel left out again.

'She'd love to,' said Mum, jumping in.

'No – we're just heading back,' I said, at the same time.

'In fact, we were just about to go for a swim ourselves,' said Mum.

So I went for a swim with the girls. As we hurtled across the hot sand, I remembered I was wearing my old navy-blue swimming costume, which Olivia had already sneered at, while the other girls had pretty tropical colours. But there was no way I could ask Mum for anything new when we had no money.

We dropped our towels and bags in a heap on the beach.

'Race you in!' shouted Charlie, tossing off her dress and sprinting down the beach.

'Last one in is a warty toad,' said Olivia, dashing after her. The rest of us wriggled out of our clothes.

'Watch Charlie's legs turn into a tail when she dives underwater,' joked Cici. 'She'll disappear in a flash to her coral palace.'

I giggled. With her shimmering green

swimming costume and long, wavy hair, Charlie really did look like a mermaid. Olivia turned a series of graceful cartwheels along the water's edge.

'Does that mean Olivia will turn into the evil sea witch?' I sniped.

Cici and Meg looked shocked.

'Olivia's really lovely,' said Meg, sounding disappointed in me. 'You just need to get to know her.'

I, of course, felt like a criminal.

'Let's join them,' said Cici, changing the subject. 'It looks divine.'

We all dived under a rolling green wave. The water was cool and invigorating, washing away the grime and, thank goodness, the grumps.

Cici shrieked as Meg splashed her. Olivia did a backflip, spraying water over everyone. Charlie splashed me, so I threw water back at her. We squealed and laughed and jumped and dived. It was nice to see the girls again, even if they were with the Evil Sea Witch Olivia.

~~~~~~

Back at the caravan, Mum had her plans spread out over the dining table and was making lists of jobs to be done. I was lying on my narrow bunk trying to read one of Mum's old books that I'd found in the cottage. It was about a group of seven kids who formed a special club. They had secret meetings in the garden shed and had all sorts of fun adventures together. I thought wistfully of how lovely it would be to belong to a club of best friends.

I say trying to read, because of course it was impossible to concentrate. Bella and Harry were lolling on the floor playing a game that involved a lot of roaring, gnashing of teeth and toy dinosaur battles.

Mum pinched the bridge of her nose as though she had a headache. Luckily, we were rescued. Mimi poked her head inside the caravan door.

'I'm feeding the chooks,' she said. 'Does anyone want to come and help?'

'Me. Me,' shouted Bella, shooting to her feet. Harry jumped up too, scattering dinosaurs all over the floor.

'What about you, Pippa?' asked Mimi.

I shook my head. 'No thanks, Mimi. I want to finish my book.'

'You can come and help us cook dinner in a little while if you feel like it,' offered Mimi.

'Maybe later.' Mum had been so busy working lately that Mimi and Papa were doing all the cooking. They were really good cooks, but I kind of missed the meals my mum made.

I tried to finish my book, but even with Harry and Bella gone I couldn't concentrate.

With Mum spread out at the table, there wasn't much room, so I moved to lie on Mum and Bella's bed. I tried to draw but I didn't really feel like that either. There was a huge, heavy rock in the bottom of my stomach.

Homesickness came over me in a big wave. I missed my old life. I missed my own room, my goldfish, Bromley House school, my London friends . . . I missed my dad.

'Are you all right, Pipkin?' asked Mum. 'You seem a bit sad.'

I swallowed. 'I was just thinking about . . . about the girls back home and wondering what they were doing.'

'Why don't you email them?' suggested Mum. 'You can use my computer.'

So I sat up against Mum's pillows and typed.

Hi Miranda, Ava and Lily,

How's everything at Bromley? I started my new school here at Kira Cove. It's been a bit hard – trying to make friends and fit in. Everything is so different. Not just the obvious things, like being hot and sunny all the time. I never thought I'd say I miss rain!! Even the sport is different. We do kayaking or surfing instead of hockey. And I'm completely useless at it. The kids are nice but it's different from having friends that I've known my whole life.

Miss you guys so much. I wish I could come home.

Love Pippa xxx ☹

I read over my message. Thinking of everything I'd left behind made me feel like crying. In the end, I couldn't send it. It just made me sound like a hopeless sad sack. I deleted the email and started again. I tried to make the message sound more like the old me. The me they'd known in London. The cheerful, chatty, fun me.

Hi Miranda, Ava and Lily,

How's everything at Bromley? I just started my new school here at Kira Cove. I've met some awesome new friends, but of course I still miss you guys loads. On Friday we went kayaking for sport (no hockey here!!). We were paddling out into the ocean and found ourselves surrounded by a pod of wild dolphins. They were so amazing. Kira Island has the most beautiful beaches – it's like living in a postcard!!

How are Captain Jack and Angelique?

Wish you guys could come and visit for a holiday. We'd have the best fun ever.

Love Pippa xxx ☺

Reading the new email made me feel a bit better. I added some photos of us swimming at the beach, outside the boatshed and having dinner on Mimi and Papa's patio. A few minutes later a message popped up on the screen from Miranda. Of all the girls, she was my closest friend back home.

Hey Pippa,

Great to hear from you! You lucky thing. The photos look amazing!! What a gorgeous place. Everything is the same here. It's been raining for a week!! Nothing else to report except we lost the hockey on Saturday. Captain Jack and Angelique send you loads of bubble kisses! Miss you. ☺

Love Miranda xx

I read her email over and over again. Getting Miranda's message made me think about my new school and the kids here. I'd known my London friends since we were tiny. We knew each other so well that our friendships were like comfy old clothes that you slipped on and immediately felt good in. But I didn't feel like I was fitting in here so well.

How could I change things? How could I make Olivia like me?

Then I had a brainwave. A plan to fit in at school. At recess and lunch, I wouldn't talk about my life back home in London. I would keep out of Olivia's way and not put my hand up in class. I would try to be super-quiet, which is hard for me. But if I didn't talk, I wouldn't stand out. I wouldn't be different. It was the perfect plan!

CHAPTER 9

THE PERFECT PLAN

On Monday I stuck to my program. I was so quiet that Meg asked me if I was feeling all right. Olivia just seemed to ignore me, which was better than her making nasty remarks.

At recess, we all sat under the big tree together. I sat as far from Olivia as possible and was so silent that I'm sure the girls forgot I was there. Everyone talked about their weekends and I didn't breathe a word. Olivia was telling a funny story about her pool party on Saturday, which only reminded me that I hadn't been invited.

After recess, we had the weekly maths quiz.

Mrs Marshall handed out the papers and told us to begin. At first, I raced through the paper, answering the questions easily. Towards the end, there was a bunch of harder questions. I chewed my pen, thinking.

Suddenly I thought back to last week, when I had topped the class. I remembered the way Olivia looked at me as if I were something nasty she had discovered. Was that why she hated me – because I'd beaten her in maths? Olivia had been really nice to me, right up until Mrs Marshall praised me.

This gave me an idea. What if I did really badly in my test? What if I didn't try at all with my schoolwork? Then Olivia wouldn't have any reason to hate me. I could fit in with the group.

I looked back over my answers. Quickly, I changed a few to make them wrong. Then I left the last three problems blank. I spent the rest of the test time doodling in the margin of my paper, drawing pictures of witches with pointy hats flying on broomsticks. One had a face remarkably like Olivia's and one looked just like Mrs Beecham.

As usual, we swapped papers with our neighbour to be marked while Mrs Marshall read out the answers. I corrected Charlie's and, like last week, she had made several basic mistakes.

Charlie handed back my paper with a frown. 'You got a few wrong this week.'

Even though I had deliberately tried to do badly, I felt a wave of disappointment. I shrugged as though I didn't really mind. 'Oh well.'

'The funny thing is that it looks like you had the right answer for some of them and then you changed your mind,' said Charlie, looking puzzled.

'I was probably distracted,' I replied.

Mrs Marshall collected all the papers and skimmed through the results.

'Congratulations, Olivia,' she said. 'You had full marks, which is fantastic. Top of the class again.'

Olivia shot me a triumphant look. She whispered happily to Sienna and Willow next to her.

Mrs Marshall handed out the papers. She paused by my desk. 'Is everything all right, Pippa?'

I flushed. 'Yeah. I mean yes, Mrs Marshall.'

'You don't seem to be paying as much attention today,' said Mrs Marshall. She looked really disappointed in me. 'Please come and talk to me if you're having any problems.'

Olivia looked extra-thrilled. Somehow I felt worse than ever. The plan to fit in wasn't working so well.

Things got worse after lunch when we had our science group. Charlie brought along the artwork for the cards she had designed, featuring four endangered African animals – the lion, elephant, gorilla and addax. She'd done an amazing job. Charlie had also researched lots of fun facts about her animals.

Cici had started writing up the rule book for the game and had scribbled down some ideas for challenges. Meg had researched her animals and made a list of suggestions to save them (don't buy lion skins, elephant paw ashtrays, or ivory pendants!!!).

I brought along . . . nothing. I'd completely forgotten about it over the weekend because I had been so busy working at the boatshed and feeling sorry for myself.

Cici stared at me in horror. 'But Pippa, you made the to-do lists. You were going to design the board.'

'I . . . I . . .'

'We can do it now,' said Meg, the peace-maker. 'We've got time.'

'But we want to do well in the science

competition,' said Cici. 'That means all of us have to try super-hard.'

Everyone looked at me with such disappointment.

'I'm so sorry,' I said, looking and feeling miserable. 'We were working all weekend at the boatshed and I completely forgot.'

'Never mind,' said Charlie. 'Let's keep going – we need a name for the game. How about "Save the Animals"?'

The others began discussing ideas for names. I kept silent.

'"Jungle Survivor",' said Meg. 'Or "African Adventure"?'

Cici grinned. Her usual good humour had returned. 'How about what we always call Meg? "Wildlife Warrior"?'

'I like that one,' Charlie said. 'It has a good ring to it.'

We worked on the cards until the bell rang for lunch.

The class streamed out into the playground. I followed the others to the tree and chose a spot on the outskirts of the group.

Olivia was already seated in her usual position, right in the centre like a queen bee. She looked me over as I sat down. I wondered if I had dirt on my face or a button missing.

'So, Philippa,' began Olivia, 'I didn't know your mother was a builder?'

I flushed. Olivia had a way of making me feel embarrassed and angry and upset all at the same time.

'She's not a builder,' I said stiffly. 'She was a stockbroker. But she's working on the building site while they renovate the boatshed.'

'Ooooh. From stockbroking to cafes? That's a big change,' said Olivia. 'How about your dad? What does he do?'

'He's not here,' I replied. I felt sick. I really didn't want to talk about Dad with Olivia.

Olivia pulled a little face of surprise. 'Doesn't

your dad live with you?' she asked. 'Why not? Where is he?'

My eyes filled with sudden, hot tears. I jumped up and mumbled something about going to the bathroom. I spent the rest of lunchtime skulking in the library, trying to look up facts about lions and elephants. I liked the library, but despite the distractions, all I could think about was Olivia and her not-so-friendly questions.

CHAPTER 10

GREEN GLOOP

After school I found Bella and Harry and hurried them out of the playground. Bella tried to resist, wanting to say a long goodbye to every single one of her friends. I grabbed her hand and marched off to the boatshed before anyone could talk to me.

'Hi, darlings,' said Mum, as we walked through the door. 'How was your day?'

Bella chatted about everything that had happened to her at school. Then Harry added a few comments. I didn't say much.

'Good news – the new oven arrived today,' said Mum. 'So I'm baking my first batch of muffins.'

'Yum,' said Harry. 'They smell great.'

They did. The warm, sweet aroma wafted through the boatshed.

'I've set up a table outside on the jetty so you can do your homework here while I finish up,' said Mum.

I sat on the jetty, drawing ideas for the board layout. Bella didn't have any homework so she wandered upstairs with Mum to watch the plumbers. Harry finished his spelling quickly and raced off to kick a football in the park with some friends.

When I was happy with my sketches, I took them upstairs to where the builders were working.

'Hi there, Pippa,' said Jason, as I came over. 'Do you need something?'

'Yes, please, Jason,' I replied. 'I was really, really hoping you could help me. I need some timber offcuts, some glue, paint and perhaps some plastic pipe for our school project.'

I showed Jason my sketches for the game board.

'No problem at all, Pippa,' said Jason with a grin. 'There's glue and paint in the storeroom. Plus I have a huge bin out the front that is brimming with offcuts. Help yourself, and let me know if you need me to cut anything to size.'

The bin was a treasure trove of timber, sawdust, smashed tiles, newspapers and pipes. I found a large rectangle of plywood, which Jason cut down to the right size with an electric saw. He set the plywood up on the table for me.

I used a black felt pen to draw the game layout on the plywood, sketching out the mountain plateaus, the wide savannah plains, lakes and a river winding down to the sea. Players had a choice of paths that took them from the flat top of the mountain all the way down to where the river joined the sea.

I grabbed empty egg cartons from the kitchen and glued them on one side of the board, building them up towards the centre in a mountain shape. I covered these with layers of newspaper strips soaked in glue, to make papier-mâché.

While the mountain was drying I started setting up the paints for the board. I had yellow for the desert sand, pale-green for the savannah grasslands, dark-green for the wetlands, cobalt-blue for the river and lakes, and deep-navy for the sea.

I was so engrossed in my task that I jumped with surprise when three heads popped around the door. It was Charlie, Cici and Meg. They'd changed out of their school uniforms into shorts and T-shirts.

'Hi, Pippa,' they chorused, crowding around the table.

'You've started making the game board,' said Charlie. 'It's looking brilliant.'

'Thanks,' I said, smiling with relief. I showed them the design sketches and how I planned to lay it out on the board.

'I love the way the players start up in the mountains and move down towards the sea through all the different landscapes,' said Meg.

'We can glue plastic animals on different parts of the board to show where they usually live,' I explained.

'Shall we help paint the board?' asked Cici.

'Sure,' I replied, handing them each a paint-brush and pointing out which sections of the board were to be painted which colour.

The girls began dabbing at the savannah plains and the desert. Cici wandered off and came back with a handful of sand. 'We can sprinkle this on the wet yellow paint to make the desert more textured.'

'Great idea, Cici,' said Meg. 'This game is going to be brilliant with us working together!'

Meg's comment reminded me of how I'd let the girls down by forgetting to make the board over the weekend. And that reminded me of all the other things that were going wrong in my life. I blew my hair out of my eyes with a little huff.

Charlie put her paintbrush down in the dish of yellow paint. 'Are you all right, Pippa?' she asked with concern. 'We were worried so thought we'd pop by and check up on you.'

'Oh,' I said. I felt a prickle of tears.

'You were really quiet today,' said Meg. 'We wondered if anything was wrong.'

The girls all looked at me.

'I didn't have a great day today,' I admitted. I paused, thinking about what to say. 'I've been feeling really homesick and worrying about the boatshed and school.'

Charlie gave me a hug, her silver bracelets jangling. 'That's awful, Pippa – but things will work out, you'll see.'

Her sympathy made me feel a little better.

Cici looked shamefaced. 'I'm sorry I got cross about the science project today. But you've made a brilliant board now.'

'That's okay,' I said. 'I shouldn't have forgotten.'

With four of us painting, it took no time at all. When the paint was dry, we could outline the pathways with black marker pen and label the challenge and query squares.

Behind us was the familiar sound of hammering, sawing and cheerful shouts. The sun glittered on the water and the air smelt of tangy salt and seaweed. I felt happy and content working with the girls on our project.

Mum came out carrying a tray. There was a plate of muffins and four jam jars filled with liquid the colour of green tree frogs.

'Hi, girls,' said Mum. 'I thought you might like to try my corn-and-bran muffins.'

'Thanks, Jenna,' chorused the girls.

Mum handed us each a jar from the tray.

'Er, Mum, what's this?' I asked suspiciously, sniffing at the gloop.

Mum beamed. 'I've been doing some research on the internet. One of the hot new cafe trends is green smoothies made with seaweed! They're super-healthy and packed full of nutrients. This recipe is made with seaweed, broccoli and spinach . . . or I could have used dandelion leaves.'

'Great,' I said, with a smidge of sarcasm. 'Seaweed-and-broccoli smoothies. Who'd have thought?'

Mum bustled off back to the kitchen. We sat on the edge of the jetty with our feet dangling over the water.

I took a tiny sip of my drink. It tasted just like it looked – slimy and bitter and salty.

The other girls drank too. They glanced at each other, not saying anything. Meg went to take another tentative sip.

'Stop,' I cried. 'You can't drink that. It's disgusting!'

The girls all burst out laughing.

'It tastes kind of … *fishy*,' said Charlie, wrinkling her nose.

'Not even our resident hippy-mermaid is keen,' said Cici.

Charlie tossed her long, blonde hair. 'Forget dandelion leaves. Give me a chocolate milk-shake any day.'

'Who thinks up these trends?' asked Cici. 'Seaweed smoothies? What's wrong with mango?'

Everyone peered at the plate of muffins.

'Shall we brave it?' asked Meg.

I took one and broke off a chunk. The muffin felt ominously heavy. I nibbled slowly at the edge.

'What's the verdict?' asked Charlie.

I pretended to gag. 'Tastes like sawdust. Even the seagulls would refuse to eat these.'

Meg jumped to her feet. 'Let's feed them to the fish. They're not fussy.'

We stood on the jetty, throwing chunks of muffin into the water. In a moment a school of silvery fish darted over. They thrashed and squabbled below, gobbling up the soggy crumbs. Seagulls swooped above our heads hoping to catch a morsel. A clumsy pelican landed on the railing and watched us curiously.

Just then a large muffin sailed out of an upstairs window and landed with a loud plop in the sea.

'Looks like the builders aren't keen on them either,' I said, gloomily.

Charlie gently nudged me with her shoulder. 'You might have to help your mum rethink the menu for the cafe,' she said. 'I don't think the kids at school will be lining up for seaweed-and-sawdust muffins for afternoon tea.'

I grimaced, feeling rather guilty, as if I were betraying Mum. 'I know. Mum's a good cook at home, but she's never run a cafe before.'

'She'll get the hang of it,' said Meg.

I hoped she was right. When all the crumbs were gone, we tipped away the green gloop and sat swinging our legs, discussing a very important topic – our favourite flavour of muffin.

We couldn't agree which was best – blueberry (Charlie), orange and poppy seed (me), or apple and cinnamon (Meg).

'They're all delicious,' said Cici, the baking queen. 'But definitely *nothing* can beat banana and choc chunk.'

I felt warm and happy sprawled with the girls on the jetty and gazing out over the cove. The sky was streaked with rose and mauve as the sun slowly sank. I was certain that this was going to be a much better week.

CHAPTER 11

WEEKEND WOE

My dreams of a long, lazy weekend were shattered when I was woken super-early on Saturday morning. Bella was stomping around the caravan, pretending to be a dinosaur. I pulled the covers over my head. 'Bella. Be quiet! Let me sleep.'

'*ROOAAR*,' Bella replied, thrashing her green *Tyrannosaurus rex* tail. 'I'm starving and I'm going to eat *you* for breakfast.'

Mum pulled the covers down and kissed me on the forehead.

'Wake up, Pipkin. We have a massive day today.'

'Noooo,' I groaned. 'I just want to go back to sleep.'

'Come on, sweet pea,' soothed Mum. 'Come and have some breakfast.'

I'd been hoping I might be able to draw or see the girls or lie in the hammock in the garden reading a book. But no. Mum had plans that involved painting shelving.

My grumpy mood only worsened as I climbed out of bed and slipped on Bella's collection of plastic beetles, which of course were scattered over the floor. Harry was sitting at the breakfast table, doing homework. Then I realised that he had used some of my sketches as scrap paper for his maths working.

I grumpily poured some muesli into a bowl, only to find a huge black spider spilled out with the cereal. Thankfully I realised it was plastic!

One of Bella's pets. Her last obsession had been jungle animals but now she'd moved onto creepy-crawlies.

'Bella!' I stood up with my hands on my hips. 'Mum, Bella's been hiding insects in the muesli again! And Harry ruined my drawings.'

Mum gently plucked the spider out of my breakfast and returned it to Bella. Then she rescued my sketches and piled them on top of the cupboard.

'Why do we have to live in a mess?' I asked. 'Why do we have to live in this horrible caravan? And why do we have to spend all weekend working on that awful shack?'

'Stop complaining, Pippa,' said Harry. 'And besides, if you hadn't left your paper all over the dining table I wouldn't have used it.'

Mum sighed patiently. 'Just a few more weeks, Pippa. It's saving us a fortune to stay in the caravan. Please don't be difficult. I really need your help today.'

Difficult? I'm not the one that's being diffi-cult! I'm not the one roaring and stomping and thrashing either!

I huffed off to Mimi's house to have a shower and get dressed. Sharing the tiny space with my whole family was really driving me crazy, especially as my sister spent half her life being a ferocious *Tyrannosaurus rex*. And I didn't think it could possibly be much better in a few weeks either – we'd be moving from a caravan to a shed!

Papa drove us to the building site. The back of his station wagon was loaded with paint tins, drop sheets and boxes of tools. He was coming to help us but Mimi stayed behind. She said she would come later when she'd finished feeding the chickens.

We were all dressed in our oldest clothes and Bella, Mum and I tied our hair up in peasant scarves. Mum suggested it might be safer if Bella didn't wear her dinosaur tail.

There were no builders about on the weekend so the boatshed was peaceful for a change.

Mum wasn't wrong. It was a massive day — sanding, sweeping, undercoating and painting. Bella's job was to help Papa and Mum by passing them brushes. Harry and I were painting the shelves for the bookshop area, under the eagle eye of Papa.

He showed us how to load the brushes so that the paint didn't drip too much and how to cut in the edges first before filling in the middle section. Despite my earlier grumbling, it was actually very satisfying to see the shelves turn a pure, glistening white.

At lunchtime, Mimi came down to the boatshed with a picnic basket laden with ham, tomato and cheese rolls, icy-cold drinks and a thermos of hot tea.

'Look at you all,' said Mimi, her eyes crinkling with merriment. 'You look like my speckled hens.'

I realised we were all spattered with splodges of white. Bella, Harry and I showed Mimi everything we had done.

'It is absolutely fantastic,' said Mimi, as she inspected the progress. 'You've done a brilliant job.'

'They certainly have,' said Papa. 'The kids have worked like troopers.'

We beamed with pride.

'Have you decided what to call the cafe?' asked Mimi.

Mum shook her head. 'I can't think of anything. Maybe Jenna's Cafe and Bookshop?'

'You need something really catchy,' said Mimi.

'How about The Boatshed?' suggested Harry. 'Or Kira Island Cafe?'

Cafe Catastrophe more like it! I thought to myself.

'Mmm, maybe,' said Mum. 'Let's go and eat.'

Mum had set up a table and chairs in a shady

corner of the jetty. We sat down and ate our picnic, chatting happily.

'You're getting there,' Papa said to Mum.

Mum rubbed her forehead. 'It's all just taking so much longer than I thought.'

She looked tired and pale. 'I had planned to send invitations out on Monday. The opening date is less than two weeks away now. But it looks like the cafe will never be ready.'

Mimi reached over and hugged Mum.

'Just send the invitations out as planned,' said Mimi. 'There's nothing like a deadline to make things happen.'

~~~~~~

Mum did send out the invitations on Monday as Mimi suggested. So the countdown was on. Ten days until the launch party.

But somehow this only made things go from bad to worse. The next few days were disastrous. One of the carpenters, Dan, fell and hurt his back, so Jason was a worker down. All the timber finally arrived on Tuesday, but now the book delivery had gone missing. The coffee machine arrived too but had been damaged in transit so a new one had to be sent for.

'You can't have a cafe without a coffee machine,' wailed Mum. 'Not only that, I don't even have a barista anymore.'

A barista is the specially trained person who makes all the coffees and does the fancy patterns on top. Mum says a good barista is worth their weight in coffee beans. It turns out the guy Mum had hired had rung on Wednesday to say he had been offered a better job on the mainland.

This was just over a week before the cafe was supposed to open. Apparently there weren't that many specialist baristas on a tiny island like Kira. Mum was almost at her wit's end. It looked like all our hard work would be for nothing.

CHAPTER 12

DOODLE DISASTER

Meanwhile, at school, life went on.

It was Thursday afternoon, and nearly time for the end-of-school bell. We were supposed to be doing maths, but everyone was feeling restless and ready to go home.

I was doodling on a scrap of torn paper. Mrs Marshall was out the front, scribbling on the whiteboard, explaining how to do a maths problem. I drew a picture of her with numbers all around. I liked Mrs Marshall. She seemed stern but was actually very kind.

She was thin, with brown hair in a bob, and today she wore a blue shirt and a skirt. When she explained maths she always came alight with enthusiasm, so I drew her with both arms up in the air and a big smile on her face. I'd finished my sketch and started on another doodle, when Charlie noticed it.

'Hey,' whispered Charlie, picking it up. 'That's really cool. It looks just like Mrs Marshall.'

Under the desk, she secretly showed it to Meg. 'Isn't it good?'

Meg passed it to Cici, who gave a muffled giggle. Alex was next to Cici, so he wanted to know what was so funny. In a moment the sketch had disappeared down the line of desks. I felt a moment of worry. I had never meant to show the sketch to anyone – it was just a doodle to pass the time.

Joey guffawed but quickly stopped. An excited whisper sounded from Sienna. Mrs Marshall whipped around. She seemed to have eyes in the back of her head. Or perhaps she just sensed a change in the energy of the room.

She stalked over to the end of the line of desks, where Olivia was sitting.

'What is it that's so funny, Olivia?' asked Mrs Marshall. She looked down at Olivia's balled fist.

Olivia shrunk down in her chair. 'It's nothing really . . .'

'May I see it, please?' said Mrs Marshall. My tummy clenched with anxiety. It must be my drawing.

Olivia slowly and reluctantly handed over the scrap of paper. Mrs Marshall examined it.

'Did you do this, Olivia?' asked Mrs Marshall.

Olivia shook her head vigorously. 'No, I didn't . . .'

'Who drew this?' demanded the teacher, her gaze raking every student in the class. She looked furious. A few eyes turned to me.

Olivia's eyes gleamed as though she was happy I was about to get in trouble.

Feeling absolutely sick, I slowly raised my hand. 'I drew it, Mrs Marshall.'

'Philippa Hamilton, I am very disappointed in you.' Mrs Marshall's tone was icy. 'Please go to the principal's office to explain yourself.'

I stood up shaking. I'd never in my life been sent to the principal's office. Mrs Marshall stooped over her desk to scribble a note and popped it in an envelope.

'No doubt Mrs Black will be calling your parents about this behaviour,' said Mrs Marshall, handing me the envelope. 'Please give this note to her.'

I couldn't bear it if the principal called my mother. I'd die of shame. And Mum really didn't need any more problems right now. She had way too many already.

With heavy feet and a heavier heart, I trudged to Mrs Black's office. I had only been there once, on my very first day.

Just then, the final bell sounded through the corridors. I knocked on the office door, dreading the rush of kids out of the classrooms. Everyone would see I was in trouble.

'Come in,' Mrs Black boomed. I scurried inside.

She was sitting behind a huge desk, dressed in her namesake colour. The desk was covered in piles and piles of papers and books. She looked rather annoyed to be interrupted.

'Yes? It's Philippa, isn't it?' asked Mrs Black, crisply. I nodded, too frightened to speak. I was clearly in deep disgrace. But I didn't think it was such a terrible crime to draw Mrs Marshall. Perhaps doodling was regarded as far more serious here in Kira Cove?

'Mrs Marshall sent me to see you.' With trembling hands, I passed her the envelope.

Mrs Black opened it and read the note, then examined my drawing, which had been tucked inside.

'Could you please tell me, Philippa, why you think Mrs Marshall is a devil?'

'What?' I squeaked. 'Devil? I don't think . . .'

Mrs Black showed me the drawing. It was the doodle I had drawn of Mrs Marshall, but someone had added to it. Someone had scribbled devil horns, a long forked tail and a wicked pitchfork. Her face had been changed so the eyes and smile were pure evil.

My heart started thumping faster. No wonder I was in so much trouble. I could feel tears prickling at my eyelids, threatening to spill over.

'I didn't do that . . . I mean, I did draw Mrs Marshall . . . but I didn't draw her as a devil,' I stuttered, my words tumbling over themselves.

Mrs Black looked at the drawing more closely. 'I see. Perhaps you can tell me exactly what happened?'

So I explained how I'd doodled Mrs Marshall being excited about maths, and how I hadn't meant for it to happen, but the sketch had been passed along the line of students.

As I explained, I thought of Olivia giving Mrs Marshall the drawing and that gleam of pleasure. Perhaps it was Olivia who had added the devil horns and tail to my picture? Perhaps she had done it just to get me in trouble? I wouldn't be the teensiest bit surprised!

'All right, Philippa,' said Mrs Black. 'I believe you are telling the truth. You can go home now and I won't call your mother. But please try not to doodle or draw during class.'

I raced back to my classroom. Everybody had gone, including Mrs Marshall. Harry and Bella would be waiting for me by the front gate, wondering where I was. I grabbed my bag and dashed out into the playground.

Lots of kids had gone home, but there were still a few milling around. I was heading to the gate when I saw Olivia and Willow chatting and laughing. I bet they were laughing at how much trouble I was in.

A wave of fury rolled over me. I was so mad that someone else had made fun of Mrs Marshall and that I had to take the blame.

I marched across to Olivia and Willow, my emotions in turmoil.

'Thanks a lot, Olivia,' I barked. 'Was it you who scribbled devil horns on my drawing? Were you *deliberately* trying to get me into trouble? Thanks to you I had to go to the principal's office.'

Olivia's face flamed. 'No, of course not.'

'You're lying,' I said. 'I know you drew it – I can tell by your face.'

'How dare you?' yelled Olivia. 'It's not my fault you were silly enough to get caught doing dumb drawings of the teacher. But I'm glad you got into trouble, Princess Think-You're-So-Perfect.'

Olivia spun on her heel and stalked off.

'Come on, Willow. Let's get away from here,' she ordered over her shoulder.

Willow leaned in towards me, her green eyes troubled. 'Pippa, it wasn't Olivia who drew the devil horns. They were already there when I saw it and I passed it to Olivia.'

'Oh,' I said, suddenly deflated. All the anger seeped away. 'Right.'

That evening, after dinner on the patio, Harry was showing Mimi and Papa his new magic trick. He spread a pack of cards out like a fan, face side up. He snapped the cards back into a pack and handed them to Papa face side down.

'Okay, Papa, now deal the cards into two face-down piles.' Papa obeyed.

'Now keep dealing them any way you like. Two at a time, four at a time,' suggested Harry after a few cards had been dealt. Papa distributed the cards randomly onto the two piles.

'Now stop,' said Harry. 'So do you think you've mixed them up enough so neither of us know what order the cards are in?'

Papa nodded, his eyes bright with amusement. 'Yes. Definitely well shuffled, Harry.'

'Good,' said Harry, picking up one of the piles and handing it to Papa. 'Now let's have a race to see who can deal them out the fastest.'

Harry picked up the other pile. 'You start first. Deal your cards into two piles and I'll do the same.'

Papa and Harry raced to deal out their cards into two piles each. Papa won, of course, because he'd started first.

'Congratulations,' said Harry, with a gleam of triumph in his eyes. 'Now let's see what cards came out on top.'

With great showmanship, Harry waved his

hands above the four piles of cards, then flicked over the top card on each. The four faces were revealed – ace of spades, ace of diamonds, ace of clubs and ace of hearts.

'Tada,' said Harry. 'It's *magic*!'

'That's amazing,' agreed Mimi.

'I know how he did it,' cried Bella. 'He –'

'Bella,' warned Mum. 'Don't spoil it.'

'I can show you another one,' offered Harry, shuffling the cards like a pro. He started to perform another of his magic tricks. Everyone sat around the table watching – Mimi, Papa, Mum, Bella and I. Then I remembered that it was my dad who'd taught Harry this favourite card trick last summer. Dad had bought Harry his magician's hat, cloak and wand and helped him learn all sorts of magical marvels. The memory made me feel hollow inside.

I stood up, wandered out to the bottom of the garden and sat on the lawn under a frangipani tree. I lay back and looked up at the darkening sky, feeling sad and sorry for myself.

A couple of minutes later, Mum came out and lay down beside me.

'So, tell me what happened today,' said Mum.

'Nothing much,' I said. I thought back to my disastrous doodle and being sent to the principal and the showdown with Olivia and everything else that had happened over the last few weeks.

'I know it's hard changing schools, Pipkin,' said Mum. 'You've had to deal with a lot – selling the house, moving and now trying to make a whole new group of friends . . . And, of course, Dad.'

That's the understatement of the year! I thought. All the feelings brimmed up inside me, threatening to spill over – sorrow, anger, hurt and resentment.

She cuddled me to her shoulder and we lay hip to hip.

'I know you've been sad and worried and sometimes angry,' said Mum. 'And with such good reason. It's been a tough few months . . .'

'*Humph*,' I said in a strangled, choking kind of way. Mum handed me a tissue from her pocket. I sniffled and wiped my eyes.

'You just need to be your usual happy, kind, friendly self and things will get easier,' said Mum. 'I promise.'

Mum paused for a moment. 'Is there anything in particular that's worrying you?'

I took a deep breath. Before I knew it I had spilled out the whole story of Mrs Marshall and the devil horns, and being sent to the principal and then the argument with Olivia after school. It was a relief to tell Mum about it.

'I thought it must have been Olivia because she doesn't like me for some reason. She keeps making nasty remarks or making fun of me to the other kids.'

Mum squeezed my hand.

'That's not very nice,' Mum agreed. 'I can see why you thought it could have been her. But I do think that you owe Mrs Marshall and Olivia an apology.'

I recoiled in dismay. *Apologise to Olivia? Never!*

'She called me "Princess Think-You're-So-Perfect",' I said.

Mum laughed.

'Have you thought that maybe Olivia might be jealous of you, Pipkin?' asked Mum.

'Jealous?' I demanded. 'Jealous of what?'

'You have so much going for you, my darling girl,' said Mum. 'You're kind and clever and pretty. You're funny and make us all laugh. You've travelled the world. For a girl who's grown up in a small place like Kira Cove, you might be intimidating.'

Intimidating? Me! Now that's a joke! The thought of Olivia Grey, with her perfect ponytail, being jealous of me. I could imagine absolutely nothing less inspiring than me, lying on the grass, snivelling and miserable! The thought did make me smile, then a little giggle bubbled up.

'Have courage, Pipkin,' said Mum. 'Life has its big ups and downs, but even in the tough times, there's always a way through it.'

CHAPTER 13

COURAGE AND CUPCAKES

I thought a lot about what Mum said. 'Have courage.'

My plan to fit in at school hadn't worked so well. So maybe Mum's idea might work better. 'Be your usual happy, kind, friendly self and things will get easier.'

On Friday morning I was determined to try it. I went to school early and said sorry to Mrs Marshall and explained what had happened. It turned out that it was Joey who'd changed my drawing and he had already confessed to Mrs Marshall. He apologised to both of us, which did make me feel a whole lot better.

All morning, I worked hard at my school work, asked questions and tried to be bright and sparkly. Mrs Marshall sprung a surprise maths quiz on us, and I did my very best. Olivia still came top, but I came second. Mrs Marshall rewarded me with a huge smile and a merit card.

After lunch, everyone walked down to the cove for sport. The four of us – Charlie, Cici, Meg and I – were behind Olivia and Willow.

Olivia turned to look at me, then turned away, her nose stuck in the air. She was clearly still very upset with me.

I took a deep breath. I heard Mum's voice in my head, *have courage*.

'Olivia – I just wanted to say sorry for what I said yesterday,' I said. 'I know it wasn't you who made me get in trouble, and you're right, it was my own fault for drawing dumb pictures in class.'

There, I'd done it. She'd probably still hate me, but I felt better.

Olivia looked dumbfounded for a moment. 'Oh? Okay,' she mumbled and turned away.

Meg gave my arm a squeeze and my friends crowded around me, with big smiles.

Kayaking was fun. We raced, splashed and made jokes. Charlie and I only capsized once this time, and that was on purpose. Afterwards, we all changed into our casual clothes and milled around outside the shed. The four of us stood a little apart, chatting and laughing.

'What are you guys doing this afternoon?' asked Cici. 'Would you like to hang out?'

'Absolutely,' said Charlie.

'We could work on our science project,' suggested Meg.

'Do you want to come to my place?' I asked. 'To the boatshed?'

'Great,' said Cici. 'I want to see how it's looking.'

When we walked through the front door of the boatshed there was a strong smell of smoke.

'Something's burning,' said Charlie.

The cause was soon apparent. Mum was in the half-finished kitchen and smoke was billowing from the new oven.

She pulled out a tray of blackened lumps.

'Is everything okay, Mum?' I asked.

Mum had a streak of flour on her cheek and looked flustered. 'So silly. I forgot the blueberry muffins because Jason was talking to me about a leak in the roof. Now they're completely ruined.'

Mum tipped the charcoal lumps in the garbage bin. 'I guess I'll have to start from scratch.'

Cici skipped over to the bench and examined the ingredients scattered in a puddle of spilled flour. There were eggs, packets of sugar and flour, and lemons. The blueberries were all gone.

'Would you like *us* to bake something?' asked Cici. I could tell she was just itching to get her hands doughy.

Mum looked unsure. 'Don't worry, Cici. I can do it.'

'Cici is the cupcake queen,' Meg assured Mum. 'Her dad's a chef so she's learned from the best.'

'Do you have milk and butter?' asked Cici.

'Of course.' Mum waved towards the new glass-doored fridge that had been installed a couple of days ago.

'Brilliant,' said Cici. 'Let's get to work.'

Cici organised us like an army captain. My job was to zest the skin of two lemons and juice them. Mum sat back on a bar stool to watch us. When she thought none of us were watching her, she looked tired and worried.

Meg whisked four eggs with a fork. Charlie mixed the flour and caster sugar together in another bowl. Cici added the eggs, butter, milk and vanilla essence to the flour mixture and stirred it with a spoon.

Then I added the lemon zest and some of the juice.

'Just a dribble more juice,' suggested Cici. 'Save the rest for the icing.'

When the batter was ready to Cici's satisfaction, we spooned it into colourful patty cases on two baking trays. Mum popped them in the oven and set the timer.

The last job was for Cici to mix the lemon icing while the rest of us cleaned up. This involved licking various wooden spoons, the bowls and eating every drip before we washed up.

Twelve minutes later, the timer rang and Cici pulled out two dozen golden-brown cupcakes. They smelled delicious.

While they cooled we worked on the game board, drawing in the tracks with black marker and numbering each space. Then we glued the animals onto the board. Our game was nearly finished.

Once the cupcakes were cool, we smeared them with zesty lemon icing.

The builders were thrilled when we carried them upstairs. I was glad that we'd saved a tray in the kitchen because the whole lot disappeared in seconds.

'Thanks, girls. You're lifesavers!' said Jason, taking a third cupcake. Dan gave us a thumbs-up sign because his mouth was crammed full.

By then, Mum was in the storeroom, unpacking a box of apple-green coffee cups and saucers that had arrived by courier. She was checking each one to make sure nothing had smashed or cracked.

'*Tada*,' I cried. 'Taste one, Mum. They're fantastic.'

The girls crowded in around me, eager to see Mum's reaction.

'Lovely, girls, but you enjoy them,' said Mum, sounding distracted.

'Mum,' I said firmly. 'You have to try one. It's important menu research.'

Mum took a cupcake from the plate and took a tiny nibble. 'Mmmm.' She took another bite. 'This is scrumptious.'

'I told you, Cici is the cupcake queen,' I said. 'We have to get the recipe for these, Mum. They'll be a mega-hit at the cafe.'

We took a plateful out onto the jetty. We sat as before, swinging our legs off the edge and eating cupcakes. We joked and chatted about our week, the other kids at school, our families and our lives.

It turned out that Charlie had a menagerie of animals at home – two border collie dogs called Zorro and Bandit, five chickens, a cat called Trixie, two donkeys called Archie and Clementine, and a baby lamb called Maisie. With five children and all those animals, their place must be total chaos!

'So yesterday after school, the five of us were lying on the kitchen floor playing Monopoly,' said Charlie. 'But Daisy had left the back door open. Suddenly Maisie trots in, stands in the middle of the board and starts eating all the Monopoly money.'

I giggled at the image of a lamb in Charlie's kitchen gobbling up the game.

'We were scrambling around trying to save everything and catch Maisie, who was jumping around like a jack-in-the-box,' continued Charlie. 'Then Zorro and Bandit race in to do their sheep-herding job, chasing her round and round the kitchen, barking like mad. All the noise brings Archie and Clementine, who are always super-curious, and they stroll right into the kitchen too. So Mum walks in to find five kids, a lamb, two dogs and two donkeys all crammed into the kitchen.'

'What did she say?' I asked, wondering how my mum would cope with all those mischievous animals. With absolute horror, I was sure.

'Mum looked around and asked if anyone had seen Trixie, because she was missing the party!'

We all roared with laughter.

'This is fun,' said Meg. 'It's been nice meeting up just the four of us.'

'We should do it more often,' said Cici. 'Maybe we should get together every Friday after school?'

A thought came to me. I remembered Mum's book about the kids who belonged to a club of special friends.

'I have an idea,' I said, sitting up straight. 'Why don't we start our very own club? Just the four of us?'

'What sort of club?' asked Meg, wrinkling her nose.

'A secret club, where we meet once a week after school and talk about things and plan adventures,' I said. 'We could have a special place where we hang out that no one else knows about.'

Charlie looked at me. 'Do you mean like a book club? Or a music club?'

I shook my head, hoping the other girls wouldn't think it was silly.

'No – more like a friendship club.'

'Like a best friends club?' said Cici.

I could feel bubbles of excitement fizzing in my tummy. 'Yes.'

'What would we call it?' asked Meg.

'Best Friends Forever?' said Charlie with a laugh. 'BFF!'

'How about BB club?' said Meg. 'Best Buddies club?'

'Or GGG – Glam Girls Gang!' suggested

Cici. She smoothed back her glossy, dark hair and struck a model's pose.

Cici made us laugh. She was such a performer. I was sure she'd be a famous rock star one day.

'I think that description might apply to you, Cici,' said Meg. 'But I'm not sure about the rest of us!'

We looked around at each other. Choosing a name was harder than I'd thought.

Just then I heard Mrs Beecham's voice coming from inside. 'Your builders are blocking the path,' she said. 'It's simply not acceptable. People have to walk there.'

Mum's voice came back. I could tell she was trying to sound patient. 'Sorry, Mrs Beecham, but we're just unloading some more timber. It won't take long.'

'How long do we have to put up with this?' demanded Mrs Beecham.

'Just a few more weeks, I hope,' replied Mum, soothingly.

'A few more weeks? You hope?' The voices trailed off.

Mrs Beecham's ranting reminded me of her comments last week, about me being sassy.

'Maybe we could be the Sassy Girls? Or Sassy Sisters.' I told them about what Mrs Beecham had said.

'Sassy?' asked Meg. 'Isn't that kind of bad?'

'Mum says that being sassy is really a compliment,' I explained. 'Sassy girls are bold and brave, and full of happy spirit – just like us.'

'I love it,' said Cici. 'Sassy Sisters it is!'

CHAPTER 14

SASSY SISTERS

I grabbed some paper and we wrote down ideas for rules, club roles and meeting places. After much discussion, joking and the occasional disagreement, we came up with the following rules for our club.

Sassy Sisters Rules!!!

- Meetings will be held on Friday after school, at 3.30pm SHARP.

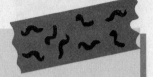

- The purpose of Sassy Sisters meetings is for four fab girls to celebrate fun and friendship.
- All members are expected to attend every week and take it in turn to supply yummy treats (seaweed and sawdust not allowed!).
- Members should strive to follow the Sassy Sisters' motto: 'Be bold! Be brave! And be full of happy spirit!'
- Under no circumstances can members blab Sassy Sisters' secrets.
- Members will take it in turns to host meetings and to hold club positions.

Sassy Sisters members and current positions:

- Charlotte Amelia Harper, President
- Megan Grace O'Loughlin, Vice-president and Research Officer
- Cecilia Mee-Shen Lin, Treasurer and Chief Cupcake Baker
- Philippa Elizabeth Hamilton, Keeper of the Notebook

Secretly, I thought I should have been the first president. It was my idea, after all, and I came up with the sassy name and motto. But I guess the other girls have known Charlie longer. I was also a teensy bit disappointed that we didn't have a special clubhouse, like a tree house or an abandoned shed.

But most of all, I was super-duper excited. I loved the idea of belonging to a special club with my new best friends. I wondered what sort of fun and adventures our gang would have together.

'So, I declare this the very first meeting of the Sassy Sisters,' announced Charlie. 'Does anyone have any business they'd like to discuss?'

Meg turned to me with a serious face. 'Is everything all right, Pippa? You seemed really sad the last few days. I know you were upset yesterday when Mrs Marshall thought you'd drawn her as the devil, but I thought it might be more than that?'

Meg is the quietest of the four of us, but sometimes I think she sees more than everyone else. She seems to have a secret antenna that lets her know when people are worrying about something.

I played with the hem of my T-shirt. I thought about pretending everything was all right but then the thought of sharing my worries seemed so wonderful. I took a deep breath.

'It's the boatshed,' I said. 'Mum has promised the bank that we will open in less than a week. But there's still so much to do. The building work ran late, and so many things were delayed, I can't see how we can possibly open on time.'

Cici and Charlie nodded.

'What happens if you don't open on time?' asked Cici.

A bubble of panic rose up in my tummy. 'I don't know – but Mum is definitely worried. She's trying her best but I don't think she can manage everything that needs to be done,' I said. 'It is so important that the business is a success. Mum's put every penny we have into starting a new life here.'

'Why did your mum decide to leave London to come to Kira Island?' asked Charlie.

Tears welled up. I hadn't talked about this with anyone outside my family. It was just too painful.

'Don't worry, Pippa. You don't have to talk about it if you don't want to,' said Meg.

I scrubbed my eyes. 'No, it's okay.'

I thought back to that terrible day. The day my world was turned upside down. The worst day of my life.

'It was my dad,' I said. 'About three months ago, he came home and told us that his investment business was bankrupt and all our money was gone. Worse than that, he said he was leaving to go and start a new job in Switzerland.' It felt like a relief to actually say it. 'Basically he said he didn't want us to be a family anymore. We had to sell our house and leave our schools.'

'That must have been awful,' said Meg. 'Do you talk to him at all?'

I nodded. 'He rings us but the calls are pretty awkward. None of us really know what to say. He hasn't called us for a couple of weeks now.' The hurt was still so raw.

Charlie gave me a hug. 'I remember when my parents got divorced. I was only little but it was terrible.'

Charlie must know exactly how I was feeling. Somehow it comforted me to know that I wasn't the only one whose family had been broken apart.

'Mum didn't know what to do,' I continued. 'So then she had this crazy idea of moving back to Kira Island where she grew up and starting "Cafe Catastrophe".'

'Not a crazy plan,' said Cici. 'A really *clever* plan . . . as long as she doesn't serve seaweed or dandelion smoothies. *That* would be a catastrophe!'

That made me laugh, in a hiccuppy sort of way.

Charlie threw her long hair over her shoulder and looked around at us all. 'You know we can all help you, Pippa,' she said. 'We're your friends. So we care about you and your family.'

'Absolutely,' said Meg.

'That's lovely,' I said. 'But I'm not sure how you can help.'

'We can have a working bee tomorrow, where everyone does odd jobs,' said Charlie. 'My family would come along.'

'We'd have the place ready in no time,' added Cici. 'Just like in the home makeover shows. My mum and dad would love to help too.'

I felt a buzz of hope. 'Really? Would you all do that for us? That would be wonderful.'

'Let's make a plan,' said Charlie. 'A plan for the Grand Boatshed Makeover!'

CHAPTER 15

THE GRAND
BOATSHED MAKEOVER

At first light on Saturday morning, Mum, Harry, Bella, Mimi, Papa and I arrived at the boatshed wearing our oldest clothes.

The horizon and sea were stained a stunning rose-pink. Mum unlocked the door and we stepped inside.

The boatshed was quiet and shadowy and strangely empty. There were no longer any holes in the floor or walls. The doors didn't hang at crazy angles anymore. Just inside the front door on the left was the bookshop nook with its whitewashed shelves, and then the space opened up into a huge room.

Golden light seeped in where the builders had put in wide picture windows along the wall. A window seat had been built underneath to take advantage of the glorious views.

On the opposite wall, the open-plan kitchen, storerooms and bathrooms had been built.

Now we just had to transform this empty, echoing shed into a beautiful cafe.

Mum set down her box of tools. She had a long, long list of jobs that needed to be done, together with concept plans and her scrapbook of ideas and photos.

'Right,' she said, looking around. 'First job on the list is to . . .'

A head stuck around the door. It was Jason, followed by the other builders, Dan and Miguel. 'I know we don't usually work on weekends, Jenna,' said Jason. 'But with your opening party next week, we thought you might need some extra hands. We need to get those bathrooms tiled.'

'Can't have a big party with no bathrooms,' added Dan.

'Oh, how lovely of you all,' said Mum. 'Come in. Come in.'

Next to arrive was Cici with her parents and brother, Will. Cici's mum, Nathalie, was carrying her sewing machine and some bolts of material. Cici's dad, Eric, carried an esky full of food. After all the greetings, Nathalie showed Mum her selection of material.

'I thought I could make you some cushions,' said Nathalie. 'Cici tells me you were planning on using lots of ocean-blues and sea-greens. Do you like any of these colours?'

Mum beamed as she stroked a roll of cobalt-and-white patterned fabric.

'That's so kind of you, Nathalie,' replied Mum. 'The colours are perfect.'

Nathalie set up her sewing machine on a trestle table and began stitching a dozen cushions for the window seat in bright, beachy colours.

Meg and Jack arrived with their mum, followed a little while later by Charlie with her whole family of five kids, and both parents, Jodie and Dave. There was a hubbub of introductions and greetings and exclamations.

I was really curious to meet my friends' families.

Mum looked around with astonishment. For a moment it seemed as though she had no idea what to do with all these people. Then she snapped to work and began organising everyone.

'Eric, could you please take charge in the kitchen?' suggested Mum. 'Pippa tells me that you're a chef so I'm sure you have some fabulous ideas on how to set it up. The kids could help you.'

'Absolutely,' said Eric. All twelve of us helped Eric unpack boxes of cutlery, glasses, saucepans, pots and jars as well as piles of turquoise and white crockery. These were neatly stacked according to Eric's precise instructions.

'I have two old wooden ladders, which I wanted to suspend from the ceiling just here, to hang the copper pots from,' said Mum. 'What do you think?'

Eric looked up at the kitchen ceiling. 'How about you hang them over to each side? Then they're not in the way.'

'I can hang the ladders,' said Papa. 'Just show me exactly where.'

Charlie's mum, Jodie, had brought a briefcase filled with paints, brushes and paper. It turned out that Jodie was a graphic designer. She volunteered to design and paint signage for the cafe – name signs, menu boards and table numbers.

'So what are you going to call the cafe?' asked Jodie, as she set up her paints.

Mum laughed. 'Pippa gave me a great idea for the name.'

I looked up from washing the glasses, my heart sinking. 'What idea?' Surely Mum wasn't going to call it Cafe Catastrophe!

Mum winked at me. 'I think Pippa called it "that awful shack" – but I thought the "Beach Shack" has rather a nice ring to it.'

'The Beach Shack,' I repeated. My heart swelled with pride. 'I like it.'

In keeping with the shack theme, Jodie painted rustic fence palings and offcuts of wood. She even did some gorgeous paintings for the walls of mermaids, fish, octopus, seagulls and starfish on weathered timber.

Dave helped with hammering, framing and hanging them on the wall.

Three hours later, just when I was starting to think we were nearly finished, two delivery vans arrived. Mum had sweet-talked them into a special Saturday delivery. The vans were loaded with an assortment of wooden tables, wicker chairs, several comfy armchairs and two sofas. Everyone helped to carry furniture and set them up according to Mum's floor plan.

'I want the sofas and armchairs grouped over here near the bookshelves and coffee tables,' directed Mum. 'Then the cafe tables go there next to the window seat, with the wooden chairs on the other side.'

Obediently we carried chairs and tables, and placed them where they should go. Mum used a measuring tape to make sure they were evenly spaced.

Jason, Dan, Miguel and Papa mysteriously disappeared but returned some time later. They carried in a huge, long refectory table that Papa had secretly built in his shed. It was made from hundred-year-old timber that had been polished until it glowed a warm, honey colour.

'Surprise,' cried Papa. 'I know you wanted a long table but couldn't afford one just yet, so I thought I'd build you one myself.'

'Oh, Dad,' cried Mum, her eyes shining with tears. 'It is so beautiful. That's what you've been doing hiding away in your shed for days. I can't believe it.'

The table was carefully placed in the centre of the boatshed with wicker chairs down either side.

'Speaking of tables,' said Papa, 'I think it's time we had a rest and something to eat. I'm starving!'

Everyone found a spot to sit – the adults at one end and the twelve kids at the other.

Mimi had made piles of chicken-and-lettuce sandwiches with lemon mayonnaise. Eric handed around bowls of homemade pork dumplings that he'd steamed on the stove. Mum pulled bottles of juice and ginger beer from the fridge.

The food smelled delicious and we were all starving after a morning of hard work. We chatted and laughed and ate and drank. It was fun to get to know the siblings of my friends – Jack, Will, Seb, Oscar, Sophia and Daisy.

After lunch, the boys washed up while Charlie, Cici, Meg and I helped Mum and Mimi to create a garden out the front.

'Every cafe needs a herb garden,' said Mum. 'But ours is going to be a little different. Ours is going to be in a boat!'

'You mean the rowing boat we rescued from the rubbish pile?' I asked.

'Exactly,' said Mum.

The six of us carried the old rowing boat and set it out on the jetty near the entrance.

Mimi had loaded the station wagon with plants, potting mix, fertiliser and pots of all sizes and colours. We filled the big plastic pots with earth. Under Mimi's careful direction we planted them with basil, oregano, parsley, coriander, rosemary, thyme and chives. Others were filled with salad greens, lettuce, tomato plants and spinach. The pots were then wedged inside the rowboat with the taller plants at the back.

Bella sprinkled all the plants with a watering can.

Around the entrance to the boatshed, Papa and Dave placed the larger pots, which were glazed sea-green, indigo-blue and coral-white. In these we planted lemon and lime trees, banana palms, orchids and tropical foliage.

Meg's mum had brought along an old brass ship's bell that she'd discovered on the ocean floor. Papa hung it near the kitchen. He also draped the rescued crab pots and fishing nets on the outside walls as decorations.

As the sun was dipping behind the mountains, we hung a dozen silver lanterns in the old frangipani tree out the front near the esplanade.

At last, it was done. Everybody helped to pack up the tools and empty boxes. Nathalie placed the last feather cushion on an armchair, and packed her sewing machine away. Mimi swept the floor.

Then we all stood in the middle of the boatshed and looked around. Everyone was exhausted and grubby.

The transformation was incredible. On the left as you walked in was the cosy lounge area nestled between the snowy bookshelves. To the right was the kitchen with its wide marble benchtop and teal-blue tiles. Further along on the left was the long window seat and the row of tables and chairs with views of the beach.

Past the kitchen on the back wall was the staircase that led upstairs, then the storeroom and bathrooms. Big sliding doors opened at the far end onto the outdoor area of the jetty, where there would be more tables and chairs.

'Thank you all so much,' said Mum. Her voice was choked up and emotional.

'I can't believe how much we achieved in just one day.'

Of course, it wasn't quite finished. We still had no books and no coffee machine, no staff and no customers. But we could see now how it was going to look. We were nearly there.

As the light faded, the other families called out their farewells and good lucks, and headed off home.

Mum, Mimi, Papa, Harry, Bella and I stood in the shed gazing around, one more time.

'Come on,' said Mimi. 'Time to go home. I think we all need a long, hot bath and an early night. We'll need all our energy to get ready for a hugely fabulous launch party.'

CHAPTER 16

FINAL COUNTDOWN

On Sunday afternoon, Meg, Charlie, Cici and I had drawn and painted a pile of posters inviting people to the Grand Opening Party. Cici and Charlie both had guitar lessons after school on Monday, so afterwards we all met at the boatshed to complete stage two of our mission. We wanted everyone to know that the Beach Shack was nearly ready to open.

We walked around the village sticking up posters and dropping some more invitations to local shopkeepers. We put posters up at school and at the surf club.

One of the last places we visited was the delicatessen. The shop was filled with the aroma of meats, cheese and wonderful spices.

A girl of about eighteen stood behind the counter, in front of the big wheels of creamy cheese, piles of salami, ham and mortadella sausage. She had long, red hair tied up in a messy bun, blue eyes and silver hoop earrings.

She smiled at us in a friendly way. 'Hello, girls. How can I help you? Would you like some chorizo? It's on special today.'

'We're not actually here to buy anything,' I replied. 'My name's Pippa Hamilton and my mum is opening a new cafe in the old boatshed down on the beach. We're having a grand opening party on Thursday and I wondered if we could please put up a poster in your window?'

The girl wiped her hands on her apron and took the poster to read it. 'That sounds fun.

I've been wondering what all the activity was down at the boatshed.'

'The cafe's looking fantastic,' said Charlie proudly. 'We all helped to set it up over the weekend.'

'My family only moved here a few weeks ago and we've been renovating it,' I said. 'But it's nearly finished now. Mum's hoping that lots of the locals will come along to celebrate.'

The girl came out from behind the counter and stuck the poster up in the window with sticky tape.

'I've only been here a little while too,' she said. 'I moved to Kira Island for a working holiday before I start university. Does your mum have any jobs going?'

'I'm not sure,' I said, my mind ticking. 'Mum did have a barista lined up, but he's disappeared to another job on the mainland.'

The girl's eyes sparkled with interest.

'I used to work in a cafe back home and I can make a brilliant coffee,' she said. 'I can even do super-cute love hearts in the froth. I'm Zoe, by the way.'

Zoe seemed like a really lovely girl. I was sure Mum would like her. And we might just have solved another of Mum's problems . . . the problem of the Disappearing Barista!

I beamed at Zoe. 'Come along to our party on Thursday and see Mum. I think she'd love to meet you.'

~~~~~

On Tuesday afternoon, the books finally arrived.

I unpacked them from the boxes and stacked them on the shelves. No one else was about, so I actually had fun flipping through the books and reading the blurbs on the back. I found at least ten that I was keen to read.

I suddenly realised that someone had come into the boatshed. Of course, we weren't officially open for business yet but I felt responsible to represent the family while Mum was gone.

I jumped to my feet to welcome the visitor. I quickly lost my smile when I realised who it was. It was our crotchety neighbour, looking cross as usual.

'Oh, Mrs Beecham,' I said, thinking quickly. I bet she was here to complain about something. *Why did she always look so grumpy?* Suddenly, I remembered what Jason had said about Mrs B having a heart of gold, and Mimi saying she didn't hate kids, she was just lonely.

Mrs Beecham looked around the boatshed curiously. It had obviously changed a lot since she was last here a few days ago. 'Where's your mother? I need to speak to her.'

I decided to try a different approach with our neighbour. I remembered that Mimi often said it was much easier to catch flies with sugar than with vinegar. I smiled a dazzling smile at Mrs Beecham.

'Please, come in, Mrs Beecham,' I said. 'I'm sorry, Mum isn't here right now, but can I make you a cup of tea?' Mimi always said a cup of tea can fix most problems.

Mrs Beecham looked taken aback for a moment. 'Oh. Yes. That would be lovely.'

'Why don't you take a seat just here,' I said, showing her to a comfortable armchair near the bookshelves. 'Do you take milk or sugar?'

'Just milk, please.'

I'd made enough cups of tea with Mimi and Mum to know that I should warm the pot, spoon in the tea, add the hot water, then let it brew for a few minutes. I carried the teapot to the table with one of the pretty, floral teacups and saucers on a tray.

As I passed, I noticed a plastic container on the bench that had one of Cici's lemon cupcakes in it. Heavens knows how that had escaped Jason! I popped the cupcake on a plate and added a fork, then carried it to Mrs Beecham's table.

'Well, thank you, Philippa,' said Mrs Beecham. 'That is very kind of you.'

'You can call me Pippa,' I said. 'Nearly everyone does.'

'Thank you, Pippa,' said Mrs Beecham. She took a sip of her tea, then a tiny forkful of cupcake. She closed her eyes. 'Exquisite.'

I sat down in the armchair next to Mrs Beecham and chatted to her while she drank her tea.

The super-friendly approach seemed to be working.

'I'm sorry about the other day, Mrs Beecham,' I said. 'But you see, my friends were trying to teach me a dance that we're learning for school. And I was completely hopeless at it.'

'A dance?' asked Mrs Beecham. 'You were practising a dance on the esplanade?'

I nodded. I wasn't sure if it would make any difference but decided to keep trying. I was hoping that I could win Mrs Beecham over so that she would be our friend, rather than our foe.

'The whole class has been learning it for months, but I only started learning a couple of weeks ago.'

'Show me,' ordered Mrs Beecham. Her tone suggested that she was used to being obeyed.

Feeling totally self-conscious with no music and no friends to copy, I began the first few steps. I hummed the song and tried to remember the routine, then gave up. I pulled a 'told you so' face.

Mrs Beecham nodded. 'I see. I think it's delightful that your friends would help you like that – and that you would dance on the esplanade by the sea.'

I was very much taken aback. 'Delightful?'

'I wish I could still dance,' said Mrs Beecham. 'But my arthritis is too bad now. I was once a prima ballerina, you know.'

It turns out Mrs Beecham had danced in the opera houses of London, Paris, Sydney and New York. She'd been given roses by prime ministers and a diamond bracelet by an Arabian sheikh. When she first retired, she'd taught ballet on the mainland, but now there were days where she struggled to walk.

I warmed to Mrs Beecham, imagining her as a graceful world-famous ballerina.

'You should come to our end-of-year concert,' I said impulsively. 'We do dance with Miss Demi once a week, and we're rehearsing for a big performance.'

Then I told Mrs Beecham the story of my first dance lesson at Kira Cove School, when I'd nearly broken Alex's nose. Mrs Beecham laughed and laughed. Then she told me a story about how at one of her first professional performances, she'd been so nervous that she'd pirouetted right off the stage and sprained her ankle.

'I'll come to your end-of-year concert if you promise me to practise hard so it is worth my while,' said Mrs Beecham in her imperious tone. 'I don't want to watch clodhopping.'

I sighed, thinking of my recent performances. 'Clodhopping just about describes my dancing! I don't think I'll ever catch up.'

Mrs Beecham put down her teacup. 'You can if you really put your mind to it.'

I wasn't so sure. My doubt must have shown on my face because Mrs Beecham's tone softened.

'You know, when I was trying to learn complex choreography, I had a few tricks that might help you,' said Mrs Beecham. 'First I'd watch someone else do it, and write down the steps in a notebook. I'd practise at home every chance I got, while watching TV, drying the dishes or making a snack. And last thing before I went to bed, I'd close my eyes, listen to the music and visualise every movement before I fell asleep.'

That all sounded rather complicated but I appreciated the advice. 'Thanks, Mrs Beecham. I'll try.'

Mrs Beecham finished her tea and ate every crumb of the little cupcake. 'Thank you, Pippa,' she said. 'I've enjoyed our conversation, but now I should be off.'

I realised that I had enjoyed chatting to Mrs Beecham too. I had another thought. I dashed back to the counter and fetched one of the invitations that we had designed.

'I know Mum has been meaning to give you this, Mrs Beecham,' I said. 'We were hoping you could come along to our opening cele-bration on Thursday evening. It starts at five o'clock.'

Mrs Beecham actually blushed with pleasure. 'How marvellous. I'm not doing anything on Thursday so I should be delighted to come along.'

CHAPTER 17

THE SCIENCE COMPETITION

On Wednesday we handed in our Wildlife Warrior game. The papier-mâché board was beautifully painted in bright colours with the various animals displayed in their habitats. The stacks of cards were precisely placed and the dice ready to roll. We had done the best job we possibly could.

All the science projects were set up in the library. Mrs Marshall and two other teachers wandered around, making notes on a clipboard as they checked each one. Charlie, Cici, Meg and I waited anxiously for our turn.

'Ours is definitely the best,' I whispered to the others, as we waited for Mrs Marshall to check our game.

Charlie glanced over to the next table, where Olivia's group had set up a toy car built from recycled junk. It was made from a plastic milk bottle, with bottle lids glued onto bamboo skewers for wheels. The top was cut out to make a space for a cardboard seat. Another bottle had been cut up to make a plastic propeller, which was linked by wires to a small battery. When switched on, the propeller would spin, making the car zoom off.

'Their car looks fantastic. I wonder if it will really drive?' wondered Cici, looking worried.

'The boys' robot made from tin cans is pretty cool too,' said Charlie.

Mrs Marshall, Mrs Black and Mr Tzantzaris

paused by our game and scribbled down some notes.

Mrs Marshall smiled at us. 'Well done, girls,' she said. 'You've done an outstanding job.'

I felt excited and proud. Perhaps we really would win the school competition and be heading off to the mainland to represent Kira Cove School at the regional science competition.

Olivia, Sienna, Willow and Tash were standing nearby. As soon as the teachers moved on, Olivia examined our Wildlife Warrior game, looking totally unimpressed.

'I don't think it's *that* outstanding,' she sniffed loudly. 'Our car is much better. It actually moves.'

I stiffened, feeling mad. Olivia had clearly said this knowing that we would hear her. I felt like marching up to her and telling her what I thought of her and her silly toy car.

Sienna took a closer look. 'I think it looks really good.'

'It's a bit babyish,' said Olivia. 'I thought Princess Thinks-She's-So-Perfect was supposed to be their lethal weapon. Maybe she's not so smart after all.'

Willow looked embarrassed. 'Shhh, Olivia. She'll hear you.'

Of course I could hear her. As Olivia very well knew. But suddenly I realised that Mum was right. For some reason, Olivia was jealous of me. So I didn't march over and tell her what I thought of her. I decided to ignore her.

It took ages for the teachers to check each project and compare notes. At last Mrs Black picked up the microphone and called everyone to attention. I had butterflies doing cartwheels in my tummy.

'Students, I wish to congratulate every one of you on your outstanding efforts in the year five science competition,' said Mrs Black in her booming voice. 'But unfortunately we can't send all of you off to represent us at the regional competition.'

She paused and read her notes.

'So, to the winning entries. As the runners-up team, we have Alex, Joey, Rory and Sam with their robot . . .'

Everyone clapped. The boys whacked backs and gave each other high fives.

'Then,' continued Mrs Black, 'for the winning team we have Olivia, Tash, Willow and Sienna for their battery-powered car . . .'

Everyone clapped again. Olivia, Sienna, Tash and Willow squealed with excitement. My heart sank with disappointment. Cici drooped beside me.

'I was so sure our African game was one of the best,' whispered Meg.

'And because it was so hard to choose a winner . . .' continued Mrs Black, looking around the library, 'we have decided to award equal first position to Charlie, Cici, Meg and

Pippa for their fabulous Wildlife Warrior game. These three teams will represent Kira Cove Public school at the regional science competition on the mainland. Congratulations to you all.'

Cici, Charlie, Meg and I looked at each other in disbelief. Then we leapt into a huddle of flailing arms, hugs and jumping up and down.

'We did it,' cried Meg.

'Hurray,' yelled Charlie.

'Great work, team,' called Cici.

I couldn't say anything for a moment because I had a mega lump in my throat. 'I can't believe it.'

I looked over and caught Olivia's eye. She glared at me.

I smiled in return. On my way back to class I stopped beside Olivia's table. The four girls looked at me nervously. You could tell they thought I might be angry about what Olivia had said.

'Congratulations,' I said. 'Your toy car is awesome.'

'Thanks, Pippa,' said Willow and Tash together.

I took a deep breath.

'I just wondered if you four would like to come to our launch tomorrow afternoon?' I asked. 'We're having a big party to celebrate the official opening of the cafe.'

The four girls looked at each other.

'We'd love to,' said Sienna.

CHAPTER 18

PREPARATIONS

The next day was Thursday – the day of the Grand Opening Party. Charlie had suggested that we should meet at the boatshed early to help Mum get ready for the party after school, then get dressed there together.

Harry, Bella and I walked to the boatshed. It was bustling with activity. The builders had been working upstairs and were just packing up. They would come back for the party later with their families.

Mum and Papa were cooking in the

kitchen, so the cafe was filled with the aroma of mini quiches and sausage rolls. Mimi had made her delicious chicken-and-lettuce finger sandwiches.

Mum and Mimi had been to the markets in the morning. They had crammed iron buckets with armfuls of flowers – hot-pink, yellow and cream roses, white lilies, purple lavender, and branches of magnolia leaves. Colourful bowls were filled with mounds of lemons, limes and crispy green apples. Pineapples and watermelon were piled on platters. The cafe looked magical.

We helped Mum to arrange the flowers down the centre of the long table and on the kitchen bench. Harry and Bella prepared candles, while I set up glasses and drinks.

A few minutes later Charlie and Meg arrived, carrying their bags. Then Eric and Cici walked in carrying cardboard boxes of something mysterious.

'What have you brought?' I asked Cici.

'It's a welcome present,' said Cici. Her face shone with delight. 'Dad and I got up super-early this morning . . . to bake!'

We all crowded around as Eric placed a pile of boxes on the long table. Cici opened the top box with a dramatic flourish.

'We have cupcakes!' she announced, revealing dozens of different-flavoured little cakes. 'Mango and coconut, lemon and raspberry, carrot and walnut, pink vanilla and . . . chocolate pupcakes!'

'Pupcakes?' I asked. 'What on earth are they?'

'The best!' replied Cici. 'Chocolate cupcakes with puppy faces on them! I know how much you love dogs.'

She showed us the tray with a variety of different puppy faces made of brown, white and black icing. They had chocolate buttons for eyes and nose, and pink candy buttons for ears and tongue.

'*Totally* adorable,' said Charlie. They certainly were.

'And totally delicious,' added Meg.

'Oh, Cici!' I cried, and gave her a big hug. 'No one has ever given us such an amazing present.'

'Thank you, Eric,' said Mum, her eyes glistening with emotion. 'And you too, Cici. You are both wonderful.'

We set out the cupcakes on trays for the party. I couldn't wait to try the pupcakes. Actually, I couldn't wait to try *everything*!

When all the food and drinks were set up it was time to get dressed. I thought we would be changing in the storeroom as usual.

'Why don't you girls get changed upstairs?' suggested Mum. She had a twinkle in her eye that meant she was up to something.

'Upstairs?' I asked.

'Let's go take a look,' said Mum. We climbed up the stairs, carrying our tote bags of clothes.

Yesterday, the builders had installed a new wooden staircase with handrails and no holes in the steps.

Upstairs, it took me a moment to realise what was different. The builders had begun erecting the walls to divide the huge space into separate rooms.

Mum pointed out what each room would be.

'This will be our living room and kitchen, overlooking the sea,' said Mum. This space was light and airy, with floor-to-ceiling glass doors opening onto a balcony that floated above the cove.

'The bathroom is next to the stairs.' Mum waved across the hall. 'My bedroom will be there in the middle, while Harry and Bella have their rooms on the landward side at the end of the hall.'

Harry and Bella's rooms were framed up with wooden posts but the plaster walls hadn't been erected yet. The only rooms that had real walls were on the seaward side. Mum pointed to a doorway leading off the hall. She smiled at me.

'I thought this could be your room, Pipkin,' said Mum.

'Really?' I asked. My heart gave a skip of excitement.

We crowded through the open doorway. It wasn't a big room. Not as big as my room in London. The floorboards were bare and the plasterboard walls unpainted. But after sharing the caravan with my mother and my siblings, it felt wonderful to think of having my very own space again.

A window had been cut into the outside wall, giving a wide view of the beach and the boats bobbing in Kira Cove. But best of all, there was the narrow ladder that led up into the tower room above.

'I get the tower?' I gasped.

'Tower?' asked Charlie. 'What tower?'

'Follow me,' I cried.

We scrambled one by one up the ladder. The tiny tower room felt crowded with four of us in there.

'Look at that view,' said Charlie. 'It's amazing.'

We could see out in every direction – the cove to the south, the mountains to the west, the village further round, the beach to the north and then straight out onto the ocean. Waves rolled in, foaming white onto the sand. Palm fronds fluttered in the breeze. Seagulls wheeled and screeched overhead. And as far as the eye could see was blue. Deep-blue sky arching overhead. Turquoise-blue shallows in the bay. And in the distance, the navy-ink of the ocean.

It really was spectacular.

'I can see our yacht by the jetty,' said Meg.

'And there's my house up on the hill,' said Charlie, pointing inland.

Cici ran to the northern window. 'You can see my house too!'

I craned my head to have a look. I hadn't been to Charlie or Cici's houses yet.

'I can't believe you have a bedroom with its own secret tower,' said Charlie.

'Well, it's not exactly a secret,' I replied.

'Yes, but none of us knew it was here,' said Meg. 'And no one can get to it unless they come through your bedroom.'

'It's absolutely awesome,' said Cici.

'I've just had the most incredibly brilliant idea,' said Charlie. 'The tower could be our secret hang-out – the place where we hold our Sassy Sisters meetings.'

'We could bring up some comfy cushions and keep our notebooks and special things here,' said Cici.

I skipped with excitement. 'That would be perfect,' I said. 'I always wanted our club to have a special place of its own.'

Our very own Sassy Sisters tower room.

When we came down from the tower the others had gone to get dressed. The girls pulled their clothes out of their bags. We all wriggled out of our shorts and T-shirts and dressed for the party.

Charlie was wearing a floaty aqua dress. Her hair flowed down her back, topped with a garland of tiny white silk roses. She wore her favourite collection of jangly silver bracelets, an anklet of turquoise stones and strappy sandals.

Cici modelled a quirky green dress with a bold print of watermelons all over it. Her fingernails were painted pearly-white and on her feet were pink ballet flats, with satin ribbons tied around her ankles.

Meg's denim skirt and blue top were less flamboyant but pretty, and she wore a necklace of crystal beads.

I had brought two dresses that had been my best ones in London, but I wasn't sure what to wear. Neither of them seemed quite right. I held them both up against me.

'What do you think?' I asked the girls. 'The navy or the red?'

Charlie was painting her toenails denim-blue. She looked up, scrunching her face. 'I'm not sure.'

'Maybe the navy,' said Meg, but from her tone, I thought perhaps the dress looked boring.

Cici rummaged in her tote bag. 'You might not want to wear it, Pippa, but I brought a dress I thought would look great on you. Would you like to try it on?'

Cici brought out a white gypsy dress with a full skirt, decorated with bands of crocheted lace.

'Are you sure?' I asked. 'It's so pretty.'

'It's one of Mum's designs,' said Cici proudly.

I pulled it over my head and twirled, enjoying its crisp coolness. It made me feel more grown-up and elegant than my old dresses.

'*Gorgeous*,' chorused Charlie and Meg.

I grinned at the girls. 'Thank you.'

'I'm not quite done,' said Cici, looking me up and down. 'I was just thinking your hair might look lovely if half was pulled back in a twist.'

Cici gathered my wild, curly dark hair and ran her fingers through it, separating it into several strands. With practised speed, she twisted the strands on either side of my face and pulled these back, then pinned the twist behind my head. The rest of my hair hung loose.

From her bag she pulled a collection of colourful glass bead bracelets and turquoise nail polish. 'Some finishing touches!'

I painted my fingernails and toenails. They were the exact colour of Kira Cove's turquoise water. The glass beads glinted on my wrist. I pulled on my white sandals.

Cici looked me up and down with approval.

'Much better,' she said with a smile.

CHAPTER 19

FABULOUS FESTIVITIES

Together the four of us walked downstairs. The gypsy skirt swished around my legs. I felt like a model walking down the catwalk.

'Look at you, Pipkin,' said Mum. Her face beamed with pride. 'You look so beautiful.'

While we had been getting dressed, the cafe had filled with people. The builders were there with their families showing off their handiwork. Zoe from the deli was discussing latte art with Mum. Mrs Beecham was chatting with Mimi and Papa, her face beaming as she nibbled a pink vanilla cupcake.

I recognised a bunch of kids from school with their parents – Alex and Rory, Willow and Sienna, Joey and Sam, Olivia and Tash. We went over to chat to them.

Alex smiled at me. Thankfully his nose was back to normal. I smiled back.

'It's amazing what your mum has done,' said Alex, looking around. 'I remember when the boatshed was abandoned. The council wanted to pull it down.'

'Thanks, Alex,' I said. 'But lots of people helped – like Charlie, Cici and Meg and all their families.'

'It's hard to believe it's the same place,' said Olivia. 'It looks really . . . cool.'

I smiled at Olivia.

Zoe came towards us, carrying a tray. 'Would you like some of Eric's pork dumplings?' she asked. 'They're absolutely fantastic, especially with the ginger soy dipping sauce.'

Everyone helped themselves, dunking the steaming dumplings in the fragrant sauce.

'Mmm,' said Cici, taking a second one. 'My favourite.'

'Thanks, Zoe, but would you like me to take these around?' I asked. 'You're a guest. You shouldn't be working.'

Zoe beamed at me. 'Actually,' she replied, 'I'm the new barista for the Beach Shack. Your mum gave me a job, starting tomorrow.'

'That's brilliant news, Zoe,' I replied.

The cafe was filled with the sound of music and chatting and laughter. Bella ran past carrying a pastry in each hand. Harry was playing hide-and-seek with some of the other boys.

When everyone had eaten and chatted and mingled, Mum rang the old ship's bell that hung near the kitchen.

'Welcome, everyone,' she said in a voice that carried right through the boatshed. 'My name is Jenna Hamilton and I'm the owner of the Beach Shack. Over the last few weeks, it seemed like an impossible task to turn this old abandoned boatshed into a cafe. Many times I felt discouraged and overwhelmed. But so many wonderful families pulled together to help us, especially the Lin, Harper and O'Loughlin families.'

I smiled at my friends. The girls stood taller.

'You welcomed us into your community, gave us your friendship and supported us through the tough times and for that I am truly grateful,' continued Mum. 'I hope that the Beach Shack will become a special place in Kira Cove for locals to gather, socialise and celebrate.'

Mum looked over at Mimi and Papa. 'Of course, I would like to thank my parents for their love and support in this crazy venture.'

Mimi blew Mum a kiss.

'Lastly,' said Mum, 'I would like to give a huge thankyou to my three beautiful children, Philippa, Henry and Isabella Hamilton.'

Mum waved us over and hugged us all close.

'These three kids have sanded, painted, hefted rubbish, sampled menus and almost *never* complained!'

Everyone laughed.

'So thank you all for coming to help us celebrate. I now pronounce the Beach Shack officially open!'

The guests cheered, clapped and clinked glasses in a toast. Everyone began talking and laughing again.

Zoe carried around the tray of pupcakes. I looked at the adorable little faces, trying to decide whether to eat a white husky, a fluffy terrier or a tan-and-brown bulldog.

'The dalmatian is my favourite,' said Zoe,

pointing to a black-and-white spotted cupcake. 'And they taste scrumptious too.'

Mum came up to me with Harry and Bella, carrying something behind her back.

'I think Pipkin might be more of a golden retriever girl,' said Mum. I looked at all the pupcake faces. I couldn't see any that looked like a golden retriever.

'I don't think we made any retrievers,' said Cici, wrinkling her nose.

'Well, luckily I have something that might help,' said Mum.

Mum held out a large gift bag. It was turquoise and green with hot-pink swirls on it. The bag wriggled and jiggled. Then it made a funny noise. A whimpering, snuffling noise.

It couldn't be, I thought, holding my breath.

'Why don't you look inside?' suggested Mum, with a mischievous expression. 'It's a surprise for the three of you to share. A present to celebrate our new home.'

Harry, Bella and I crowded around. Cici, Charlie and Meg huddled close too. Together we peeked in the bag.

A face peered back at us. It was fluffy and creamy-blonde with a black nose and brown eyes. It blinked and yawned, showing a delicate pink tongue.

'It's a puppy!' I screamed. I could barely contain my excitement. 'It's an adorable puppy.'

'Is it really ours?' asked Harry, looking at Mum in astonishment.

'Absolutely,' said Mum. 'She's eight weeks old and ready to come live with us.'

'What will we call her?' asked Bella. 'She's white – so maybe Snowy or Sugar?'

Our new puppy was the colour of Kira sand. She reminded me of all the things I loved about our new home. The sea, the beach, the endless sunshine. At once her name came to me.

'We should call her Summer, after her new home.' I looked around at my three best friends. 'She's a Kira Island girl – just like us.'

CICI'S LEMON CUPCAKE RECIPE

Makes 12 regular or 24 mini cupcakes

¾ CUP OF CASTER SUGAR

125 GRAMS OF SOFTENED BUTTER

2 EGGS BEATEN WITH A FORK

2 CUPS OF SELF-RAISING FLOUR

¾ CUP OF MILK

1 TEASPOON OF VANILLA ESSENCE

1 TEASPOON OF FINELY GRATED LEMON ZEST

ICING

1½ CUPS OF ICING SUGAR

2 TABLESPOONS OF LEMON JUICE

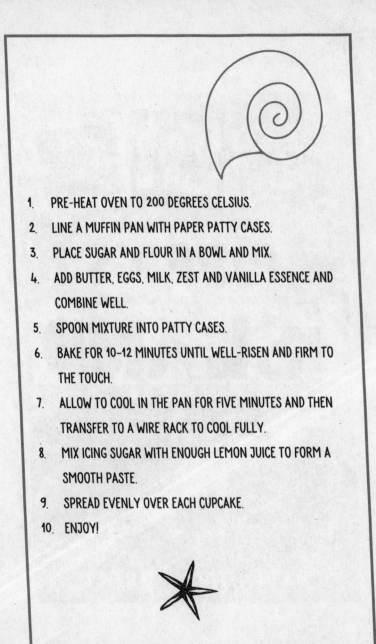

1. PRE-HEAT OVEN TO 200 DEGREES CELSIUS.

2. LINE A MUFFIN PAN WITH PAPER PATTY CASES.

3. PLACE SUGAR AND FLOUR IN A BOWL AND MIX.

4. ADD BUTTER, EGGS, MILK, ZEST AND VANILLA ESSENCE AND COMBINE WELL.

5. SPOON MIXTURE INTO PATTY CASES.

6. BAKE FOR 10–12 MINUTES UNTIL WELL-RISEN AND FIRM TO THE TOUCH.

7. ALLOW TO COOL IN THE PAN FOR FIVE MINUTES AND THEN TRANSFER TO A WIRE RACK TO COOL FULLY.

8. MIX ICING SUGAR WITH ENOUGH LEMON JUICE TO FORM A SMOOTH PASTE.

9. SPREAD EVENLY OVER EACH CUPCAKE.

10. ENJOY!

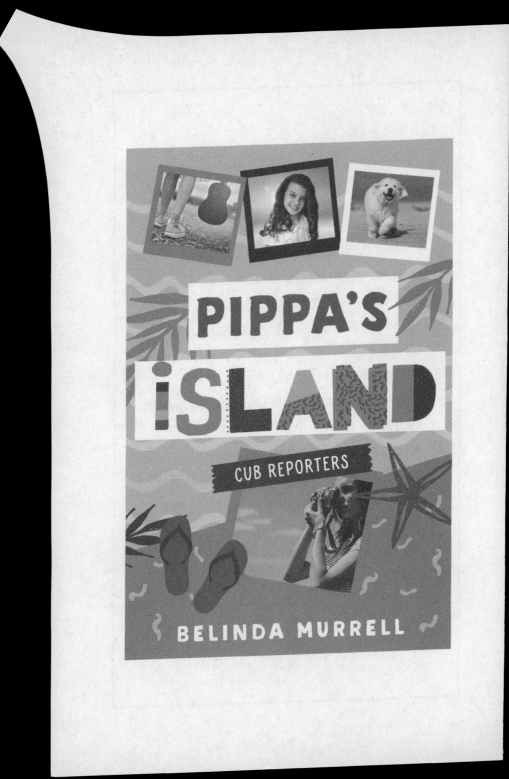

PIPPA'S iSLAND

CUB REPORTERS

BELINDA MURRELL

CUB REPORTERS

Pippa is settling in to her island home – she's even learning to surf. School is abuzz when Mrs Neill announces the launch of a new student newspaper. But how will Pippa, Meg, Charlie and Cici decide what to write about when the four friends have such different interests? A fashion photo shoot could be fun – if it weren't for bad weather, a naughty puppy and other disasters.

Just when things couldn't get any worse, the cub reporters get a news scoop that could bring the whole town together at the Beach Shack Cafe. Cupcakes for everyone!

Whose story will make the front page?

OUT NOW

ABOUT THE AUTHOR

At about the age of eight, Belinda Murrell began writing stirring tales of adventure, mystery and magic in hand-illustrated exercise books. As an adult, she combined two of her great loves – writing and travelling the world – and worked as a travel journalist, technical writer and public relations consultant. Now, inspired by her own three children, Belinda is a bestselling, internationally published children's author. Her previous titles include four picture books, her fantasy adventure series, The Sun Sword Trilogy, and her seven time-slip adventures, *The Locket of Dreams, The Ruby Talisman, The Ivory Rose, The Forgotten Pearl, The River Charm, The Sequin Star* and *The Lost Sapphire.*

For younger readers (aged 6 to 9), Belinda has the Lulu Bell series about friends, family, animals and adventures growing up in a vet hospital.

Belinda lives in Manly in a gorgeous old house overlooking the sea with her husband, Rob, her three beautiful children, Sammy the Stimson's python and her dog, Rosie. She is an Author Ambassador for Room to Read and Books in Homes.

Find out more about Belinda at her website: **www.belindamurrell.com.au**

Adventures are more fun with friends!
There are thirteen gorgeous Lulu Bell
stories for you to discover.

Love history? Escape to another time
with Belinda's seven beautiful
time-slip adventures.

If you love fantasy stories, you'll love
Belinda's Sun Sword trilogy.